ENIGMA IN WHITECHAPEL

STEPHEN A. PEASE

 **FriesenPress**

Suite 300 - 990 Fort St
Victoria, BC, V8V 3K2
Canada

www.friesenpress.com

Copyright © 2017 by Stephen A. Pease
First Edition — 2017

All rights reserved.

No part of this publication may be reproduced in any form, or by any means, electronic or mechanical, including photocopying, recording, or any information browsing, storage, or retrieval system, without permission in writing from FriesenPress.

stephenpease.com

Patricia King-Edwards, Editor
editrite@yahoo.ca
www.ca.linkedin.com/in/patricia-king-edwards-00336a9

Portage Design, Webpage Designer
www.PortageDesign.com

ISBN
978-1-5255-1363-3 (Hardcover)
978-1-5255-1364-0 (Paperback)
978-1-5255-1365-7 (eBook)

1. FICTION, THRILLERS, SUSPENSE

Distributed to the trade by The Ingram Book Company

In life, there are accomplishments and unfortunately, disappointments. In this maze of life, we all need a shining star to guide us along our way. The author was a post WWII baby, born to Canadian parents who had just gone through the hardships of the father being shipped overseas to fight in the war. When he returned, he was not the same. The war had changed him. In today's world, it's called Post-Traumatic Stress Disorder.

This book is dedicated to the author's mother, Hazel Mary Pease (1915-1966), who was eventually abandoned to raise her two children alone. She was a brave and proud woman, who did the best she could. She was a shining star.

TABLE OF CONTENTS

ONE	TOWER HAMLETS	1
TWO	THE RIPPER	12
THREE	THE OCEAN ESCAPE	21
FOUR	CANADA	30
FIVE	A BEAUTIFUL COUNTRY	43
SIX	HAPPY NEW YEAR	55
SEVEN	THE STRANGER	65
EIGHT	AN UNEASY PEACE	79
NINE	A NEW LIFE	90
TEN	THE BROTHERS	97
ELEVEN	A DEATHLY CALM	112
TWELVE	THE DEATH OF TONY	120
THIRTEEN	COME OUT, COME OUT WHEREVER YOU ARE	133
FOURTEEN	THE HUNT IS ON	146
FIFTEEN	VANISHED	159
SIXTEEN	THE TRIAL	172
ABOUT THE AUTHOR		185

ONE
TOWER HAMLETS

Henry Bruce was a relatively good man. Oh, he had his faults, but who in the East end of London didn't? He lived a modest life with his wife Emma and their two children Winifred and Roland. Emma was a pretty woman with a lovely smile attributable to her near perfect teeth. Good teeth were unusual in London where most people had unusually crooked teeth inherited from generations of generally bad teeth. She was a strict woman, not only with her children, but also with her husband as well. As a result, Henry had few of the bad habits that most of his friends had. He drank very little, never allowing himself to get intoxicated. Emma would tell him if she couldn't afford the time to be intoxicated; then neither could he.

Henry was an average looking man. Like most men who worked on the docks, he was slightly underweight from the hard work and long hours. He was muscular and very strong, though. He had been very popular with the ladies. As a young man, he had a way about him that made women want to get to know him — maybe it was his big blue eyes or his inviting smile. The only vice that Henry had was he loved the Greyhound dog races.

Emma's parents lived in a row home in the borough of Stepney. She came from a family of four, having only one brother. Not that far from where Henry and Emma lived. Emma was a talented woman who had an uncanny knack of being able to draw what she saw before her, including portraits or landscapes. She was able to make a few extra quid drawing portraits near the Tower of London.

The two Bruce children were average kids of the day, both semi-educated, like their parents. They spent their day trying to make a few pence any way they could. Winifred was twelve years old, a very sweet young lady, well mannered just like her mother. Luckily for her, she had the same dental traits as mom so her teeth were nice and straight. She had taught herself to read and write with some help from her friends; although, she still couldn't write anything on her own without assistance.

Winifred was popular with the other kids on Repton Street and enjoyed playing games on the street in front of the house. Her mother Emma would tell her to enjoy it now because in a year or two, she would have to be loaned out to a local family as a maid to make extra money. Winifred had the same artistic talent as her mother and could draw portraits, although not as well as her mother could. No doubt she would improve, as she got older.

Both Winifred and Roland were healthy children and for the most part were very well behaved. Roland was ten years old and very smart for his age. He was slightly under size, but wiry. Most of the other mothers would tell Emma she shouldn't worry about it. Like Winifred, Roland at age ten, was well on his way to being able to read. Most of his time was spent playing with friends or getting into mischief, as young boys do. He tended to be a little bit heavy handed with the other boys in the area. He had proved himself numerous times to be someone not to be tangled with. Roland's greatest pastime was watching the bare-knuckle boxing matches put on by the numerous clubs in the area. Every borough in Tower Hamlets had a club. They would meet for prearranged fights every Sunday in various places, mostly open fields or empty lots.

One club would host another for several fights between club members. The clubs had no clubhouses or gyms. The events were held for two reasons: first, to name the year's best fighter; second, as a betting forum where money could be made betting on the right fighter. Although Roland was too young to participate he rarely missed a fight that the Stepney Club was participating in. Roland watched and learned the techniques and proper methods of fist fighting. The local boys learned the hard way that he could apply these traits better than any other boy in the neighbourhood.

The area of Tower Hamlets was a very congested place. It bordered the City of London proper on the west. It consisted of twenty-six boroughs including: Stepney, Canary Warf, Limehouse, Poplar, Isle of Dogs and Whitechapel to name a few.

Immigrants moving into the area looking for work had increased the population to over a half a million people by 1880. Along with the congestion came crimes of every kind. There were thieves and prostitutes on every corner.

The year was 1888 and Henry and Emma had been married for about twelve years. Most of that time, Henry had been working at the St. Katherine's Dockyards. It had been built in 1828 on the North side of the Thames River. The dockyard was about a mile and a half from the Tower of London, and Tower Bridge.

The Bruce family had moved in with Henry's father George, at 47 Repton Street, in the Tower Hamlets borough of Stepney, a city within a city you might say. The house was a modest two-story row house with only five rooms. It was one of a hundred similar houses in the area. To say the least, it was in disrepair and would stay that way due to a lack of funds to make any improvements. This meant that the Bruces could only have two rooms to themselves. An agreement had been made with Henry's father when they moved in that this was a temporary arrangement and that Henry would seek appropriate lodgings at his earliest convenience. That had been ten years ago. Henry would pay a rental amount on the first of every month. Failure to do so would mean instant eviction.

George had lost his wife, Elizabeth, Henry's mom, several years earlier to the plague. Not a day passed that George didn't think of her. Maybe this was why he always seemed to be in a bit of a mood. She had been a very good-looking woman when George met her. They had courted for several years before getting married at St. Dunstan Church. George was an average looking man about five foot five inches and 150 pounds. Now, he was sixty-seven years old and had retired two years ago.

George had been a bit of an oddity in the neighbourhood. He was one of the few men who didn't work at the shipyards. He had been employed at the Tower of London of all places as an internal maintenance worker as well as a grounds keeper. He had worked there for forty years. Because of his good job he was able to buy the row house on Repton Street, where he and Elizabeth had raised their family. Together, they had six children of which only three survived to see adulthood. Three of them met their end due to the plague or some other disease. It was truly heartbreaking, but not uncommon in the east end of London. The other three children — Henry, Jack and Madeline all grew up on Repton Street. Henry was the youngest of the three, but all three were now married and leading their own lives. When Jack and Madeline married they moved away from London. Jack moved his family north to pursue work as a farmer. Madeline and her husband had moved to the state of Maine in the United States of America so George thought.

George was now retired. He had saved just enough money to live on for the remainder of his life. When Henry and Emma finally moved, George would have to take on several boarders. This would give him extra income. Until then the money Henry paid in rent helped George to get by.

At the dockyard Henry was employed as a tanner and blacksmith. He was proficient at his trade so, unlike most men that worked there, he was almost assured a steady income. The dockyards were a dangerous place to work at the best of times. Deaths were common and occurred at least once a week, mostly from falling cargo. Non-fatal accidents occurred with more frequency, often leaving men permanently disabled. Seeking any kind of medical attention in 1888 was next to impossible. This left those with more severe injuries to languish in the streets of Tower Hamlets as beggars.

The house on Repton Street was approximately two miles from the Tower of London and Tower Bridge. George Bruce had told stories as to the goings on at the Tower of London over the years. Mostly, about the executions that had been performed there. When he was a child, his parents would take him to witness the Beefeater Guards who were stationed at the Tower as it still housed prisoners. There had been no executions at the Tower since the mid 1700's. However, prisoners could still be found incarcerated there protected by a shroud of secrecy. Even though, George knew a lot about the Tower having worked there for forty years; he rarely talked about what went on inside. Henry's mother, used to tell her children that their father had to swear not to talk about it. George did say he felt lucky that he had no hand in the executions, *like in the good old days*, of the Tower.

Buckingham Palace was also a mere five miles from Repton Street. The contrast between the two locations was like day and night. Henry would take his family to view the Palace on Sundays after attending services at St. Dunstan's All Saints Church. They always hoped to see Queen Victoria ride by in one of her ornate carriages and on one occasion they actually did.

She was like a god to the British people, especially, to those who lived in London. To get to the Palace, one had to take a route that skirted the area of Whitechapel. This area was one of the roughest in London. It was riddled with prostitutes and other unsavoury types. The children were always instructed never to go there.

Henry was a relatively good man as stated, but he did have his weaknesses. He loved to bet on the Greyhound

Races. No, he was obsessed with betting on them. Every Saturday evening after work, you would find him at the races. At first, he was a modest gambler, only betting what he could afford to lose. As time went on, though, and his losses multiplied, his addiction grew worse. Of course, Emma could not be told, she worried enough about the money.

The dog races were relatively new. They consisted of Greyhounds chasing a mechanical hare down a straight track. This was called coursing. At first, only two dogs chased the hare, which had been given a substantial head start. After the sport adapted betting, up to six dogs raced at the same time. This provided a wider field for betting. Henry's answer to the problem of losing was to bet heavier so that when he did win he could cover his losses. To do this, he had to borrow an amount of money. This enabled him to amalgamate all his smaller debts into one large debt to one person or group. Henry chose to borrow fifty pounds from a group of men that he knew.

However, these men, well known in the Whitechapel area, were unscrupulous as well as unforgiving. Known as the Tower Gang, they were a well-organized group of thugs. It was common knowledge that they specialized in loan sharking as well as in prostitution and extortion. They were a dangerous group of men. It was rumoured that they had committed numerous murders. Henry had heard that many people had borrowed money from the gang. So long as they paid the money back on time, they had no trouble with these outlaws. If Henry's luck did not turn around in short order, his life, and possibly the health and well being of his family would certainly be in jeopardy. The gang had given Henry no more than one year to pay the debt back with interest.

The next Saturday saw Henry back at the track, ready to apply his strategy. It took him until the last four races to get the feel of the track and how the dogs were running. When the time was right, he would lay his first bet — a fairly modest one, but sizeable none the less. If he came out ahead, he would continue in the next race increasing the bet, continuing this strategy. Sometimes it worked and a nice profit could be made. Over the next six months miraculously Henry won back all that he had borrowed plus most of what he had lost prior to borrowing the money. Life was finally going to get better for the Bruce family. With the winnings, he could foresee putting a down payment on a small house and getting some of the things that his family deserved.

The first step in this reformation was, of course, to pay off the debt to the gang who had loaned him the money. He took a trip to Whitechapel and had a meeting with the Tower Gang. Rumours of a serial killer had been circulating in the neighbourhood. The murders had been occurring in the district of Whitechapel. The victims had been mostly prostitutes working the area. Police from the Tower Hamlets area as well as the London City Police were investigating. The murders had been so gruesome that the papers had nicknamed him as *"Jack the Ripper"*.

Many theories were being expressed as to who *"Jack the Ripper"*, could be. There were no suspects as yet. When questioned by the police, prostitutes related that members of a local gang had been extorting money from them. They had been threatened with disfigurement or even death, if they told the police the names of the men involved. Even the name of the gang was kept secret. The only suspect the prostitutes would talk about was a man nicknamed, "*Leather Gloves*".

The police were starting to go door to door questioning all occupants of the Whitechapel area. It took about a month before they came knocking on the door at 47 Repton Street. George Bruce was asked to provide the names of those living at the address, along with where they worked. While in the house, the police couldn't help notice the condition of the house compared to the adjacent houses. George's house seemed to be in a better state of repair compared to the others, thanks to Henry's greyhound money. The furniture was newer, and Emma, Winifred and Roland were dressed in newer clothing. The police asked questions about this, but Emma attributed the apparent affluence to Henry's job at the dockyard.

The next Sunday, the Sunday before Christmas, Henry had to meet with the men to repay the loan. He was on time at the agreed upon location, but the gang members came late. When they showed up, they seemed to be in a belligerent mood. Henry had the money in an unmarked envelope. With a smile on his face, he handed the envelope over to the main man, Jake Skinner, or "*Skinny*", as he had been nicknamed. Henry was proud of himself that he was able to repay the debt four months earlier than agreed upon. This, he thought, would save him money based on the exorbitant interest rate that he was being charged. Jake took the envelope and counted the money. "What's this then, a down payment?" Jake asked sarcastically.

"Payment in full" replied Henry.

"You've got to be bloody kidding. Are you trying to give me a blinker?"

"You're short, it's only half here." said Jake, as he stuffed the envelope of money into his shirt.

Henry's hair stood up on the back of his neck, he had heard what these men could be like.

"I've given you the agreed upon amount, plus your interest, and now you want more. You're trying to shake me down you bugger." said Henry.

"Let me make this clear to you mate. Double what's in the envelope and have it back here a week next Sunday or we pay a little visit to that pretty little wife of yours. Before you go, I want to introduce you to one of my boys, they call him, '*Leather Gloves*'," said Jake.

With that, a strange burly man stepped out of the shadows. He was a big man, over six feet tall, and broad at the shoulder. His arms were muscular with hands like meat hooks. His face was riddled with numerous scars, and his hair was long and unkempt. He was wearing leather gloves and was punching one hand with the other.

"This is Tony. He will be the one to deal with you, if I don't get my money... I'll deal with your pretty wife." said Jake.

The other gang members snickered. Tony walked up to Henry, and with one hand grabbed him by the throat, with the other he made a fist and punched Henry in the solar plexus. Henry couldn't breath, and was at the point of blacking out.

"Let this be a warning to you, mate. Do as you're told and you might get through this with your head intact." threatened Jake.

Henry was in shock. How could he have been so naive? What was he going to do now? All the way home, he thought about his situation. He had to stop once to throw up, as a result of the blow to his stomach that he had received. He knew there was no hiding from the gang. He had heard of other men who had borrowed money from them, but had never made any attempt at paying them back. These men were dealt with very severely, being badly beaten, and in one case murdered.

Henry didn't have the money they were demanding. He thought the money in the envelope had been more than enough to satisfy the gang, but it wasn't. He started to panic. He knew there was no way to get the money in such short time. There was only one answer, to leave town and get as far away from the gang as he possibly could. He had to take Emma and the kids and run.

TWO
THE RIPPER

The conundrum that Henry found himself in was that by just moving from the area of Tower Hamlets would not save him, or his family from the abuses of the gang. They had their spies everywhere. Whatever he did would be passed on to the group of thugs. He would have to create a plan to divert the gang's attention away from him and his family, while they affected their escape from the area. In the days prior to Henry's marrying Emma, he would have stayed and tried to stand up to the gang. Even now, he wasn't concerned for his own safety; it was for the well-being of his family that made him so anxious.

First, Emma would have to be told what had transpired. This would probably be the most difficult part of the plan. Henry loved his wife and children dearly, and would do anything to keep them safe. He did not want to lose them.

Their marriage was strong, and Henry had always been the dutiful husband. He had never caused Emma any reason to worry, until now. Emma had always disapproved of his betting on the dogs. She had no idea how much money Henry had ended up losing. If she had known; she would have put an end to it long ago.

The second step in the plan would be picking a destination, a safe place to run to. In reality, Henry and Emma would have to decide whether the threat was great enough to warrant a move to another country. If this were their fate; what country, what continent would they be relegated to? Money would be the deciding factor. After purchasing tickets, they would still need about twenty- five pounds to start their new life. Clothing was the only possession they could take with them – nothing else. All would be left behind.

As soon as he arrived home he approached Emma. "Me darlin, we need to talk about something very important." Henry said sheepishly.

"What are you on about now Henry, more money for the track?" Emma said jokingly.

"No luv, its much worse. I've landed meself in a bit of a pickle, you might say."

Over the next hour, Henry fully disclosed to her what had transpired. At first, Emma was shocked until the anger took over. She weighed her options as they discussed how they would handle this *'bit of a pickle'*. From what she had heard herself about the gang, just distancing herself from Henry would not make her safe. The gang would still take out their revenge on her and the kids, if they found them. Besides, she loved Henry just as much as he loved her. She decided that the only answer would be for her to continue to support Henry to the end. Emma assured Henry of her devotion to him. Even though, she was still in shock, and dismay; she leaned over and kissed him.

Decisions had to be made. The first was to decide where they would go.

They considered all of the available possibilities. One by one, the list was narrowed down. In the running was the east coast of the U.S.A., possibly New York. The other was to Canada, —Toronto, in particular. Henry believed he had an uncle that had moved to the Toronto area. Each location had its pros and cons, which were discussed at length. As they talked about the change their life was about to take, they both agreed that it was becoming exciting. As they let their imaginations take over, the more exciting it became. The voyage, the new land, settling in a new city or town, all meant a new beginning for the whole family.

Henry's uncle Thomas, who was also a tanner by trade, had moved several years ago. It would be most advantageous for Henry and Emma to find out exactly where he had moved. Then, they would consider making the same move. The only problem with this plan was trying to find out the location of the uncle. No one could even suspect what they were planning, not even Henry's father George.

Now, that the plan was coming together, Henry and Emma could start the preparations. First, Emma would discretely sell off as much of the family possessions as she could to her closest friends. This would raise some of the needed cash for the escape. While Emma was doing this, Henry set to work finding the whereabouts of his uncle Thomas. He knew that his father, George, had received a letter from him several years earlier. Henry was sure that letter would contain an update on the location where Thomas had moved to and finally settled. The letter would no doubt be kept in a travel chest in George's room.

When George went out, it would be an easy task for Henry to search the chest and locate the letter. A few coins given to George, for several tankards of ale would assure Henry the time needed for the search. Henry searched his dad's room and found the letter confirming that his uncle had in fact travelled to Toronto, Canada, where he had begun his new life. There was even an address for him. Henry then recruited his best friend, William Pert, to go and find what ship was leaving for Canada within the next week. He also asked him to purchase tickets on behalf of Henry and his family for the trip. William expressed a desire to follow with his family at a later date. This was excellent news and the two men laughed at the possibilities.

The final step in the plan was to create the required diversion to give the Bruce family the time to get to the docks and board the ship that would take them to their new destination. Once the purchased tickets were in Henry's hand, he would send an anonymous message to Sir Melville McNaughton, the head of the Criminal Investigation Department of the London Metropolitan Police Service. This message would inform them that the identity of *Jack the Ripper* was in fact a man in the Tower Gang known as, "*Leather Gloves*", whose real first name was Tony.

William had found out that the next ship leaving Liverpool at the end of the week was the White Star Line's TEUTONIC — a ship five hundred and eighty two feet in length and fifty-seven feet in breadth. She was capable of carrying three hundred first class or saloon passengers, one hundred and fifty second class and seven hundred and fifty steerage passengers. It would take six days to cross the

Atlantic and after stopping in New York, it would eventually arrive in Halifax, Nova Scotia, Canada, about ten days after setting sail from Liverpool. At first, William had been told that all the tickets had been spoken for, but if he waited, there were four tickets that hadn't yet been confirmed. William decided to wait in the lobby. After a short while, the purser called him over to say that he was able to sell him the four tickets, as they were still unclaimed. William purchased the four tickets for steerage class and then hurried back to give them to Henry.

Unfortunately, for Henry and his family, it was the middle of December 1890, which meant it would be a cold voyage to say the least. This, of course, would be exacerbated by the fact that they could only afford steerage. A steerage cabin was in the lower part of the ship so it would feel colder and damper. When Mr. Pert had been asked to purchase tickets to Halifax, Henry had instructed to obtain them for the next ship leaving London, despite the cost. As a result, William had obtained the tickets for the *Teutonic*, which was a more upscale steamer. Of course, this was reflected in the price of the tickets. The cabin was a four-birth cabin, which was perfect for the needs of the Bruce family.

The ship would leave Liverpool on the 19th of December, which gave Henry five days to put his plans in motion. Emma was doing well with her task of liquidating most of their possessions. She had already raised the fifty pounds that they would need. The children would not be told of their plans until the day the boat sailed, but they were already inquisitive having noticed that most of the family possessions were missing, Emma had just said that she had stored some of their property.

Jack the Ripper, meanwhile, had struck several more times after having taken a short break from his slaughtering ways. Two more prostitutes had been murdered and brutally dismembered over the past few days. This put more pressure on the police as the public was demanding action. What a perfect time for Henry's plan to be implemented. Therefore on the 18th of December, Henry drafted the letter to the police and placed it in an envelope addressed to Sir Melville McNaughton. William, Henry's friend, had agreed to deliver it to the police station. With any luck, McNaughton would open and read the letter on the morning of the 19th, at the same time the Bruce family were boarding the *Teutonic*.

The man known, as '*Leather Gloves*', was well known to the police. It wouldn't take them long to throw out a dragnet to arrest this new suspect. His full name was Tony Drummond and he was known in the east end as a thug and a 'molly', which was a term given to homosexuals. He also had very violent tendencies. The police would already have a lot of information about the gang so this would put them under investigation as accomplices. *What a plan*, Henry chuckled to himself. The gang would have no idea where Henry and his family had fled. By the time they found out, it would be too late for them to act. He hoped that they wouldn't pay for someone to take the next liner out to try and intercept him and his family. Henry was not only pleased, but was also proud of his plan.

Of course, Henry really had no idea who the real *Jack the Ripper* was. Maybe, he was a disgruntled patron of the prostitute scene or maybe, a truly deranged man who just hated all women. Whoever he was, Henry hoped that the police would capture him as soon as possible. Until they did, no woman in the Whitechapel area was safe. This was the first time in London's history that a murderer of such ferocity had preyed on its citizens. The magnitude of Jack's crimes would surely lead him to the gallows when he was caught. Henry hadn't really kept up to date with his crimes so he made a mental note to obtain a newspaper, dated the 19th of December to catch up. One question he had been asking himself was whether or not Jack the Ripper was acting alone.

When Henry had confided in William Pert about the predicament he now found himself in, William had offered his assistance and expressed a desire to follow Henry at a later date. The two agreed to maintain their friendship by writing to each other as often as they could. Henry and William talked late into the evening about resettling in Canada and how the move could be the best thing that ever happened to either one of them. William Pert was thirty-eight years of age and his wife Sarah was but thirty years old. Together, they had a child named Roger who was five.

Years ago, the Bruce's had helped William and Sarah out when their son Roger had become deathly ill. They had given the Perts money to take the child for proper treatment that no doubt saved his life. William and Sarah lived with her parents in a small house located in the borough of Limehouse, which was about a mile from Repton Street. William and his wife had often talked about moving out to be on their own. Life in Sarah's parent's home was tolerable, but strained. The couple knew that a move would be in order before much longer.

William also worked at the shipyards, which is where he had met Henry. He was employed as a stevedore, loading and unloading the ships. As a stevedore William had no real trade, which narrowed his opportunities when seeking employment. It had taken him ten years to attain a full time status at the docks. On two occasions, he had narrowly missed being seriously hurt on the job. Both times, the danger came from falling cargo, which had been mishandled. William disliked working in the yards so if there had been an alternative; he would have taken it long ago. The thought of working there until he died or was unable to work any longer was a sobering thought.

Since Henry and Emma's predicament had reared its ugly head, William and his wife had been talking about following the Bruces to Canada. They agreed that the move would be difficult. They were young enough, however, to start a new life in another land. Henry and William had also discussed going into business together, at some point, opening a leather shop. This would be perfect in Canada as leather was used there for almost everything. Henry could teach William the tanning trade and together they could have a thriving shop. William and Sarah had, therefore, decided to start putting money aside to pay for steamship tickets to Canada to join their friends.

Henry and Emma lay in bed on the eve of their great escape. All the plans had been made, checked, and double-checked. They talked briefly about getting up at an early hour to get Winifred and Roland ready to go. This would include informing the children about what was to transpire.

Any misgivings or change of heart was to be dealt with now. In the morning, there would be no time for discussion. Henry took Emma in his arms and kissed her with passion. He was so glad he had her by his side. She was his soul mate to be sure. In a while, both fell into an uneasy sleep. It was five in the morning, but the sun had not risen yet. It was time to wake the kids for breakfast. Then get on their way to the *Teutonic's* dock. None of the Bruce family had ever been on an ocean liner. This was going to be an experience to remember.

THREE
THE OCEAN ESCAPE

All passengers were to be checked in on board by eight o'clock in the morning on the day of sailing. Henry and his family were at the gates at seven thirty with bags in hand. They were ready for the big adventure to begin. Henry was nervous nonetheless. He was sure that on the trip to the *Teutonic's* dock, he had observed one of the Tower gang's members hanging around a nearby street corner. He felt confident, though, that they hadn't been spotted, but it was cause for concern in any event. The Bruce family hurried onto the ship and out of sight of anyone down below on the docks. They were given their cabin number by the purser and would stay behind the closed cabin door until they were out at sea. At two o'clock in the afternoon, as advertised, the ship pulled away from the dock at Liverpool. Before long the huge ship was clearing the harbour shipping lanes on its way to the open Atlantic.

The day couldn't have been nicer. The sun was shining and even though it was cold, as most days in December are, the cabin was surprisingly warm and comfortable. The sea was fairly calm and the new passengers could hear the sound of seagulls following the ship. Winifred and Roland had been told what was happening. Emma had made it sound like it was a planned event, a chance at a new beginning and had made no mention of the trouble that their father was in. They were told of the new land where they were moving to and what they could expect once they got there. The two kids were excited about all that they had been told. For now, though, they wanted to get out of the cabin and start exploring the ship. After the ship had been an hour at sea, they were allowed to do just that.

The police that day conducted several raids in the early morning hours on residences where the Tower Gang members were known to live. Of course, they were looking for Tony or 'Leather Gloves'. He had been on their watch list since the interviews with some of the prostitutes in the area of Whitechapel. The girls had related that a gang member had been extorting them and had described him. The plan had worked in that the gang was so preoccupied with the police that the last people on their minds were the Bruce family. This was a major lesson for Henry.

Never again would he put his family's lives in jeopardy. He was a changed man and would give up any type of betting in the future.

Emma and Henry took a tour of the ship to find out where all the amenities were. There were two dining areas, one for first class and one for the steerage passengers. Also of interest was the sick bay for medical treatment, the library, laundry and some facilities and playrooms for children. Information pamphlets were also given out to instruct everyone what to do if an emergency should arise. They outlined where the lifejackets were kept and what lifeboat their cabin was assigned to, their steward's name and what services they could expect.

All passengers were assured of the safe sailing record of the Teutonic and the experience of the captain and crew. The captain was Henry Parsell R. N. R. who was a man of fifty-six years old having spent most of his life at sea.

At last, the family could relax and start to make plans for their future. Over the next few days, Emma and Henry were able to discuss what they would like to do once they were settled in Toronto. Emma was adamant about the children going to school if at all possible. This had been impossible in London as the cost of an education was far too great for the Bruce's to afford, but they thought maybe things would be different in Canada.

Before leaving London, Henry had had a talk with his father George. He told him what had happened. George was concerned, but understood and offered any assistance that he could give. George was able to then tell Henry of his uncle Thomas which was of great help. Thomas was also a tanner by trade. According to George, Thomas had worked in a hotel when he first moved to Toronto, someplace called the Gladstone Hotel. George was certain that Thomas could either find Henry a job as a tanner or at least get him a job in the Hotel.

Emma had aspirations of her own. If the children could be enrolled in school that would leave Emma free to get a job of her own, something she had never had. Young girls in London had only one opportunity at work, which was to be a live in maid with another family. Now that Emma was starting this new life, she hoped she could maybe work in a store, bakery, or some other kind of interesting work. In any event, at last, the future held promise. She had also heard that land and in particular houses were cheaper in Canada. Maybe, just maybe, she and Henry could afford a house in a few years, which was something she had always wanted.

Emma and Henry had lost two children in London due to the Flu epidemic, which had been devastating for both of them. The mortality rate in London was terrible to say the least. One in five babies died within the first year of life. Although, they had been blessed with two beautiful children, Emma always regretted not having had one more. Maybe Canada would be a healthier place to have children. Emma wasn't getting any younger, at thirty-five years of age, the time for having children was quickly coming to an end.

Henry made a point of getting to know some of the other men in steerage. He was interested in knowing what lay ahead in Halifax and then Toronto. This whole situation had been thrust upon the Bruce family in such a short time that it was only now that Henry realized how little he knew about Canada let alone Toronto. Usually a man who is moving his family such a long distance has done his due diligence on the new location. The only thing that he was sure of was that Canada was a British colony with a similar type of government so they would speak English and would have the same religious beliefs. These facts put Henry at ease and confidant that he and Emma had made the right decision to move there.

He had heard that Canada was a very big country and cold. He, therefore, had many questions that he needed answers for such as how far it was from Halifax to Toronto? How would they get to Toronto and how long would it take? Where could they stay in Halifax? So many questions... Before leaving London, Henry had written a letter to his uncle Thomas. In the letter he had explained the circumstances in which he and Emma now found themselves. He explained that they were on their way so could not wait for a return letter and had no idea when they would get to Toronto. He asked if it would be all right if they contacted him when they got there. He explained that he would need to get a job preferably in his trade as a tanner.

Two days out and the Bruce family had settled in to a regular routine. The first day aboard ship was spent unpacking and becoming aware of their surroundings. Dinner had been pleasant. The family ate a good meal consisting of a form of Shepherd's Pie made with pork and vegetables. Dessert was a plain vanilla cake. For the adults, there was ale with dinner and coffee or tea with dessert. The children drank milk. The evening was spent in their cabin discussing the day's events. The children had met other kids going to Canada. After talking with them, they were even more excited about the trip. They had heard stories of the huge amounts of snow that fell every year, and how children in Canada skate on frozen lakes and ponds. This made Henry and Emma wonder if the clothing they had brought with them would be warm enough. They were sure they could afford to buy warmer coats and footwear once getting to Halifax.

Talking to some of the passengers as well, the primary topic of discussion was the mode of transportation to go from Halifax to Toronto. Henry discovered that around 1885, the Canadian Pacific Railway had completed a transcontinental rail system, which went all the way from Nova

Scotia to British Columbia. The rail line had apparently been built by blasting through huge rocks — something called the Canadian Shield. These were huge rocks left behind by the last ice age. The other passengers Henry talked with were also unsure of how long the train trip would take. Judging from the distance to be covered, they all agreed that the trip would take at least two to three days to get to Toronto. It would take the travelers up the Atlantic seaboard, along the St. Lawrence waterway for a distance, then to Quebec City and down to Lake Ontario, which it would follow into Toronto. The trip promised to be both beautiful and uncomfortable at the same time. Train rides could be cold and breakdowns were common, but the scenery would be awe-inspiring.

Wildlife apparently was in abundance all along the journey. Animals that the Bruce family had only heard of such as Moose, Black Bear, Porcupine, Coyote, Beaver and Mink not to mention the assortment of birds that would be seen. The snow-covered countryside would be like none other they had ever seen either. As an added bonus, they all spoke about Canada's clean air. This would be a pleasant change from the polluted air of London. The pollution came from the burning of coal both for industrial and residential purposes. The Bruce family had already noticed the change in the air, how it smelled so good compared to back home.

Emma too talked with the other ladies on board so was told that Canada was backward in a lot of ways, especially, when one is away from the big cities such as Toronto and Montreal, compared to London, but Emma had expected as much. She was told of the abundance of the fruit and vegetables available from local farmers and markets. She was also told that because Canada was a relatively new country the people still had a pioneering mentality, which meant most people were more than willing to help their neighbours.

Most of the ladies that Emma spoke with were going out of the Toronto area, where there was still plenty of good land available for farming. Their husbands were looking at settling land as it was very cheap to buy and a good living could be made there. Henry and Emma had never discussed this possibility, but she thought that maybe it deserved their consideration. In any event, the picture being painted for Emma was one of a beautiful country where food was plentiful and the people kind and helpful. It also sounded as if there would be no dog racing tracks!

"But what about Indians?" Emma asked in a concerned tone.

One of the other ladies answered, "Yes there are Indians, but they aren't wild like they used to be. They live in the north and really don't bother anyone."

The ladies all muttered, "Thank god!" and chuckled.

Emma also learned that Toronto had very good government run schools and universities; there was even a well known art school that Winifred could attend. Children were required to attend school at least until their sixteenth birthday. Emma also learned of the large department stores in the big cities easily accessible by streetcar. After hearing all this new information, Emma felt good about their new adventure.

While still at sea, Emma had something she had to tell Henry. So she waited until they were alone in their cabin and then told him. She said that a man in first class had made unwanted advances toward her soon after they had got under way from London. He had introduced himself as Sir Edward Cotton of Birmingham. She went on to say that he would confront her whenever he saw that she was alone in the lounge. Several times he offered to buy her a drink or at least a cup of tea, which Emma refused. He had been persistent, even though, she had made it clear that she was a married woman with two children. To this, he replied that he could do a lot for her artistic endeavours and that he knew people who would pay handsomely for her drawings and or paintings. "After all," he said, "I am very well placed with very influential friends." You and I could be really good friends, if you know what I mean. Emma told Henry she was quick to walk the other way if she saw this man coming.

Then she said, "The last time I saw him was yesterday. I was alone in the lounge when he walked in, came over to where I was sitting and started in on me again. He said he couldn't get me out of his mind and what a lovely face I had and that my body was very nice too. With that the blighter put his hand down the front of my blouse and grabbed me. I jumped up and hit him with the book I had been looking at. I screamed at him and called him every name I could think of. He seemed startled at first and then said did I know who I was talking to. I tried to kick him, but he deflected the blow. Then before walking away, he told me I was just London trash and not worth his attention."

Henry became furious. He had heard of incidents such as this with the elite class. He determined he had to be careful if he and Emma went to the captain to complain, as it could backfire on them. The word of a first class person would be taken over that of people from steerage class. As if Henry didn't have enough on his mind… this had to happen. He could not let it go, though, "this aristocratic son of a bitch had to be taught a lesson."

FOUR
CANADA

On Friday the 25th of December, the Teutonic slipped into its birth in New York City. A few hundred passengers would disembark the ship leaving only those passengers bound for Halifax. The Teutonic would spend the night at port leaving for Halifax the next morning. The weather during the Atlantic crossing had been good, but a storm was coming up from the Caribbean threatening to delay the rest of the voyage. The captain would make the decision in the morning whether to leave or not.

That night, Henry decided to take a walk on the foredeck. As Henry walked on the foredeck, he marvelled at the skyline of New York City. He had no idea how huge it was. As it was the middle of winter, steam was pouring out of the rooftops of the huge buildings in the downtown core. Emma had described her predator to him — he seemed to always wear a grey overcoat with a white carnation in the lapel. It was late now and Henry had not expected anyone else to be on deck, but there he was, the man with the grey topcoat carnation and all. He was standing with two other men and all three seemed as if they had too much to drink.

They were boisterous and seemed to laugh at anything that was said. Finally, two of the men left saying good night to their friend "Good night Sir Cotton nobleman extraordinaire" and then they went into the ship and could be heard laughing as they walked down the corridor.

The 'nobleman' didn't see Henry as he walked over to the boat railing and was looking down at the water. Henry looked around to see if anyone else was nearby. When he assured himself that the way was clear, he walked behind 'his highness' and with one hand grabbed him by the seat of the pants and lifted him up over the railing. Sir Cotton yelled as he was going down, but once he hit the water he was completely silent. It was quite a drop almost forty feet down to the water, and once there the water was frigid. If he had survived the fall, he would have to contend with the freezing temperatures of the night air and the water. Henry, though, had no intention of killing the man, as much as he wanted to, so he started yelling "MAN OVERBOARD, MAN OVERBOARD". Within seconds, sailors were scrambling around him on deck asking where the man had gone over which Henry showed them.

"He must've tried to commit suicide" Henry said.

The sailors began throwing life rings trying to save the drowning man. The officer on watch asked Henry if he knew the man, and did he see anyone else on deck when the man went over.

Henry replied "I've never seen the man before, but at the time he went over the railing, I saw a man walk quickly past this gentleman".

"Thank you, sir. That will be all and thank you for raising the alarm" said the duty officer.

"I hope the gent is ok, good night." replied Henry as he walked away.

Henry knew that 'Sir Touch a Lot' couldn't identify him so if he were asked, he would deny any knowledge of what the man had done to Emma, if that should some how be revealed.

At seven o'clock on Friday morning the 26th of December, the Teutonic was on the move again. The Bruce family could feel the swaying as they lay in their beds.

"I guess we're on our way" Henry said.

"The sooner the better" Roland said, "I want to see a Moose."

They all chuckled at the thought.

As they entered the open sea, it was obvious that it was going to be a rougher voyage than the first half of the crossing. There were ten to fifteen foot swells and the ship creaked with displeasure at being tossed by the rough seas. The ship made sounds it had not made previously which concerned the Bruces. The motion of the boat made it roll back and forth, which made walking down the corridors more difficult. In fact, it was challenging to even eat breakfast, what with the dishes sliding back and forth, not to mention the queasy feeling that comes with eating when the seas are rough. Even though, it was a very large ship; the rolling seas still affected the passengers. The Bruces wondered how people accomplished anything at all on ships much smaller than the Teutonic.

Henry joked saying, "Can you imagine how Christopher Columbus felt on the Nina, Pinta or Santa Maria?"

"You'd never see me on a small ship like that" said Winifred.

It was plain to Henry and Emma that the next few days would be spent in the lounge or in their cabin. Both places were warm and comfortable and the children could spend their time playing card games while mom and dad read the papers provided in the lounge.

Much to their surprise, Henry and Emma saw Winifred using her drawing skills while in the lounge. She was sketching on a pad when one of the other passengers saw her and asked her if she could do a drawing of her. Drawing portraits was a talent that was always in demand in Victorian times. Photography was in its infancy and was very expensive. Before long, to the amazement of her parents, Winifred had drawn over ten portraits and made herself ten shillings. Her mother told her to keep the money for her new life in Canada. Winifred insisted, though, on giving five shillings to her parents. Maybe there was an art school she could be enrolled in once they settled. Winifred, they had to realize, could even make a living drawing portraits. The future held so much promise. This move to Canada was turning into a true blessing in disguise.

While in the lounge, Henry had an opportunity to read the London Times from the 19th of December. He came across an article about raids conducted by the Metropolitan London Police on the residences of gang members in the Tower Hamlets area. These raids were as part of the investigation in the 'Jack the Ripper' murders. Several people had been arrested and charged with offenses not related to the Whitechapel murders including a man named Tony Drummond nicknamed 'Leather Gloves'. The article went on to say that the gang had been broken up so would not be of concern to Whitechapel residents in the future. This was music to Henry's ears.

When he told Emma about the gang being broken up, a discussion ensued about continuing the trip. Henry and Emma both agreed that no matter what, the move to Canada was probably the best thing to happen to the family. Even if things didn't turn out well in Canada; it was still a wise move. Besides, Roland had to see a Moose!

Emma then asked Henry if he had heard about the man from first class falling overboard the previous night. Henry replied that he had heard a commotion on deck while he was taking his walk, but really hadn't paid much attention to it, "How is the man doing?" Henry asked

"He's okay, I guess. He's been relegated to his cabin for bed rest for the rest of the trip" replied Emma.

"Oh that's too bad," replied Henry with a smirk on his face.

At about four in the morning, the Bruce family was suddenly awakened by an alarm going off and by yelling in the corridor. Henry sprang to his feet and opened the cabin door. One of the stewards was pacing up and down knocking on the doors. He was telling passengers to get their lifejackets and a heavy coat and to proceed to the lounge where they would wait for further instructions. Henry was able to get the stewards attention so asked what the emergency was. The steward replied that a fire had broken out in the boiler room and that all passengers were being instructed to go to the lounge or dining areas. As far as the steward knew, the fire was under control. It was the captain's orders to have all passengers assemble as indicated. If the danger resolved itself, after an appropriate length of time, then passengers would be allowed to return to their cabins.

While in the lounge, Henry met two of his new acquaintances and heard something very concerning from them. One of the men, who was concerned with safety aboard liners like the Teutonic, took it upon himself to do a quick count of the lifeboats aboard the vessel. To his amazement, he discovered there were too few lifeboats for the number of passengers aboard. The lifeboats could serve approximately seven hundred people; however, with a full complement of passengers and crew, there was double that number, around fourteen hundred persons all together on board. When Henry questioned one of the officers about this, he was told that the Teutonic complied with the Maritime laws of the day as set by the British Admiralty. This answer offered no sense of security to them at all.

"God help us if anything should happen" muttered Henry. He would make sure that Emma was not made aware of this concerning fact.

After an hour had passed, the captain appeared and gave a short speech. First of all, he wanted all passengers to know that any danger that had been present was now gone. In particular, the ship's boilers were in good shape and had survived the incident unscathed. He further related that because the boilers were fed with coal, occasionally, coal dust would ignite causing a flash fire of low grade and intensity. These fires occasionally happened even on the biggest and best of ocean liners; however, the crew was well trained in how to deal with them. He went on to add, "Our crew is particularly proficient in dealing with this type of emergency. Please, everyone return to your cabins and get some rest." He reassured everyone that the rest of their trip would be uneventful.

Now, that the excitement was over, the Bruce family returned to their cabin where they agreed that they would sleep in a little in the morning. Henry was still shocked about what he had been told regarding the lifeboats. He found it hard to fall back to sleep again as he worried about the consequences of a disaster at sea.

The next day, the seas were slightly calmer, but it was bitterly cold out on deck. As the Bruce family made their way to breakfast, Henry couldn't help but think about how cold the water would be. What if a catastrophic event resulted in all the passengers ending up in the water? He had heard that in really cold water, coupled with the air temperature, even the heartiest of men would only last minutes before dying of hypothermia. This was one very good reason that Henry had never had the urge to go to sea as a deckhand. If he had to meet his end, he wanted it to be in a nice warm bed at home.

The expected day of arrival in Halifax was Friday the 29th of December 1890, only two days left to what had turned out to be a long and arduous journey. Henry could only imagine what it must have been like on the smaller ships that must have taken months to make the same voyage. Thank God for new technology Henry thought to himself and also wondered what traveling across an ocean would be like in the future. He considered that probably they would make the crossing in less than a week; although, he had no idea how they would accomplish such a feat. Anyway, Henry was just grateful that ocean vessels no longer had to rely on sail power and the tacking that went with it.

Emma and Henry had decided that the family would seek temporary lodgings for a couple of days before moving on to Toronto. They all needed a good rest, which really couldn't be found aboard the Teutonic. They also had to purchase some warmer clothing, especially, coats and gloves. Henry wondered also if he could possibly obtain a map of Toronto. This would assist him in finding the residence of his uncle Thomas who lived on Gladstone Avenue, in the west end of the city.

Meanwhile, Henry had obtained the necessary Immigration cards from the purser as instructed. A card had to be filled out for each member of the family and turned in to officials in Halifax upon their arrival. On the card, they requested all of the pertinent facts of the immigrant including his or her date of birth, where they were born, marital status, occupation, address, amount of money on hand, whether he or she could read, or ever been denied access to Canada; one's next of kin, destination in Canada and next of kin in Canada. Henry thought that filling out the cards prior to docking should make the process quicker.

The rest of the trip would hopefully be uneventful and go by quickly, after all Roland wanted to see his moose. On that note, in the lounge, Roland had found a picture book all about Canadian wildlife, which he studied intensely. He would tell his mother about the beaver and bison, the moose and wild turkeys, the deer, the badgers, the muskrat and a lot of other animals they had never seen before. He also had his mother read part of a book that described how huge Canada was, and how it was many times the size of Great Britain. At one point during the trip, Roland was told by one of the other boys on board that he had seen a huge whale come to the surface right near the boat. Roland decided he was going to do some whale watching on the off chance of sighting one of the biggest animals on earth.

Emma and Winifred had a long talk about their love for drawing, which they shared. They agreed that once in Canada they would try their hand at drawing the different scenes that they would pass on their trip to Toronto. No doubt, there would be some amazing sights along the way. While staying in Halifax, they could do some drawing of that city as well, if they were there long enough. The idea was that after the trip was over and they were settled in Toronto, they could compile their work into a picture book. Emma had always wanted to try and paint a landscape, maybe this would be her opportunity to do so.

On the morning of the 29th, the family got up early and started to pack. At long last, the arduous ocean journey would be now over in a matter of hours. They could feel the excitement rise, as the ship got closer. There was a lot more activity aboard the ship what with people moving baggage about and the crew getting organized for the docking routine. Finally, someone saw land as the ship followed the coastline all the way into Halifax. This part of the trip was finally drawing to a close. Most of the passengers were anxious to get to Halifax on time, after all New Years Eve was just two days away so most people had plans to usher in the New Year. The Bruces, however, on New Year's Eve would probably find themselves riding in a train bound for Toronto.

Before they knew it, they had docked and were disembarking. They had to go through a building, which apparently housed the immigration department. Already the Bruces could tell the people here were friendly and helpful. The process went well and the officials actually talked with Henry and Emma about their upcoming trip telling them what they could expect. Henry felt good about their move, and could hardly wait to get to Toronto. First, though, they had to find lodging for the next few days and then purchase train tickets. The officials at immigration were most helpful with this as well giving Henry several tips on boarding houses and where to buy the train tickets.

As they were walking away from the dockyard where the Teutonic was birthed, Emma asked Henry. "It was you wasn't it? I mean the man falling overboard into the water?"

"Why honey, I have no idea what you're on about," replied Henry as he walked away with a grin on his face.

Henry's first impressions of Halifax were favourable. It was a clean city, with quaint brightly coloured houses set close to the harbour. All of the streets were made of cobblestone and rose away from the harbour. Finding the boarding house was an easy task, having followed the directions given by one of the immigration officers. The woman running it, Mrs. Godfrey, was friendly and couldn't do enough for the new immigrants. As they were moving into their rooms, she even showed up with sandwiches and milk for the kids. Roland was so impressed he asked his mother why they hadn't moved here earlier.

Once every one was settled, Henry thought it would be wise to walk down to the train station to obtain the schedule and if at all possible buy their tickets for their upcoming trip. Roland volunteered to go with his dad for the walk. Winifred and her mother opted to stay behind and rest. While walking to the train Station, Roland and his father had a chance to talk about this new land they were in. Henry told him how different they would find it living there. He said that Roland might find the other children a little bit different than the kids back home. His father also told him that Roland would have to remember that life here was a little harsher than in London. In London, there was safety in numbers, meaning that there, people were always around to help him if he needed it. In Canada, there were considerably fewer people so people tended to be friendlier and more willing to help anyone that needs it. Roland agreed saying he had already noticed that people in Canada were a lot friendlier and that's how everyone should be no matter where you live.

"Maybe in a perfect world Roland" said Henry.

"Dad, can we go fishing when we get to Toronto? I've never been fishing and I've heard it's a lot of fun." said Roland.

"Of course we can, I promise. I'll take you fishing as soon as the weather permits, and, we find the best place to go, okay?" exclaimed Henry.

The two had to ask for directions to the train station, which caused a fifteen-minute conversation with one of the locals. Finally, they found themselves entering the station. It was a modest wood framed building measuring approximately forty feet by fifty feet. The tracks were at the rear of the station and there was a large waiting room just inside the front door. Large wooden seats much like those in a church lined the waiting room providing plenty of opportunity to sit and relax while waiting for the train.

A counter was on one side with a gentleman standing behind it. He was answering passengers' questions and dispensing train tickets. He seemed very helpful and pleasant. As Henry and Roland walked over to the counter, the wooden floor creaked telegraphing their arrival to the railroad employee.

"Can I help you sir?" asked the attendant.

"Yes, thank you. I want to purchase tickets on the next train going to Toronto." said Henry.

"Not a problem sir. That train will leave here tomorrow the 30th at 10:00 am. Now, how many tickets will you be needing, sir?" asked the attendant.

"Four tickets, one way please." said Henry.

The transaction completed led to another conversation about where Henry and his family had come from and what it was like where they were going. The attendant was kind enough to suggest a store where the appropriate winter clothing could be purchased. Luckily, another passenger came into the station needing the attendant's attention so Henry and Roland could leave without further conversation.

They decided to head back to the boarding house to get Emma and Winifred and to take them to get some warmer clothing. The day was not, especially, cold, but it felt five to ten degrees colder with the constant wind coming off the harbour.

As Roland and his father approached the rooming house, Henry couldn't help but notice the condition of the building. It was one of the few brick homes in the area, It looked well built and must have been considerably more expensive to build compared to the other houses in the area. It looked to be only five to ten years old and was truly a beautiful building. One could only imagine what the grounds and gardens would look like in the summer months as trellises adorned the front of the house so roses would grow there.

The Bruce family shopped the rest of the afternoon, and after they were satisfied with their purchases; they returned to the boarding house ready for a home cooked dinner. They would now be warm with their new coats, boots and hats. The conversation at the dinner table revolved around the beauty and ruggedness of this new country. Henry had expressed a wish to return to Halifax at some point, as he was impressed with the beauty of the city. Then it was off to bed, after all they had a date with a train in the morning and with any luck Roland's moose!

FIVE
A BEAUTIFUL COUNTRY

The next morning, the family packed their bags yet again and after a hearty breakfast and saying their goodbyes to Mrs. Godfrey, it was off to the train station. Mrs. Godfrey had packed a lovely lunch for them, and also sent along a glass container of milk for the children. Emma thought to herself that when they finally got settled that she would assemble a basket of goodies and send it to Mrs. Godfrey along with a card expressing their deepest gratitude. Henry expressed the wish to return there one day to see what the gardens at the front of the house looked like in summer.

It was a short walk to the train station so the family found themselves sitting in the pew-like seats at 9:30am, only to find that the train would be late in leaving. Apparently, the tracks that approach Quebec City were so snow covered that the Canadian Pacific Railway - C.P.R. as it was called for short had to call out a special crew to clear the snow off the tracks. The attendant said Roland would love to see that. They had to put a snowplow on the front of the steam engine and then run down the track at full speed. The snow would go flying in the air as tall as a three-story building and all signs of the locomotive would disappear in a cloud of snow. The Bruces were told that this happens three or four times in a normal winter and twice as many times in a bad winter.

So, the Bruce family found a bench that was empty and settled in for what could be a long wait. When the train finally did arrive, the attendant announced that after twenty or thirty minutes, it would be ready to go again. At that time, they could board. Until then, there was fresh coffee on the pot-bellied stove. The room could hold about one hundred passengers, but by ten o'clock there were approximately thirty people waiting. According to the attendant, the train held fifty passengers; if for any reason there were more passengers than that, an extra car would be added to the train.

While Henry was talking with the attendant, the attendant let slip that C.P.R. trains only ran on time in the summer so long as they didn't hit a Moose.

Delays in the winter months were normal, and could result in hours being wasted. Normally, the trip to Toronto took twenty-four hours, but if delayed, the trip could take two days and on occasion three days; if the weather was extremely bad. Henry told the attendant how the trains in London prided themselves on their punctuality, and then quipped that they didn't have moose to contend with.

Henry couldn't help but think back to the reason that had taken them so far from home. He wondered if he had got away with it; if the gang would really give up. Things were actually going too well and he always had the feeling that at any moment '*Leather Gloves*' would come walking through the door. He decided that he should have a back up plan in the back of his mind, just in case. In his paranoia, Henry thought that he and his family would be safe for now, at least until they got to Toronto. Once in Toronto, he would buy himself a gun at the first reasonable opportunity. He could explain the ownership of the gun for hunting purposes. He then had to resign himself to the fact that he would really have to use the gun should the need arise. Could he actually shoot someone? Henry would only know the answer to that question when it actually happened, he prayed to God the day would never come.

All of a sudden, the doors leading to the tracks swung open and a man they assumed was the conductor yelled "ALL ABOARD". And with that, passengers started climbing up the steps into the train cars. The Bruce family made its way inside the car and down between the seats to the first set of four seats that were available. A rack above their seats could accommodate their luggage or at least most of it, the rest would have to go under the seats. The seats themselves were comfortable with lots of legroom.

The coach seemed brand new, as it showed no signs of wear or abuse. It took a while for the car to warm up as it had had the doors at each end left open for so long, but they could feel the heat coming back into the coach. There were about fifteen passengers in this car, which would hold about thirty- five when it was full. All in all it was very comfortable.

"Oh my!" Emma exclaimed, "I just realized that this will be your first train ride Roland."

The boy nodded his head and then said, "I'm hungry!"

Emma reached for the bag that Mrs. Godfrey had so kindly prepared for the Bruces and then declared, "Let's see what we have here." She started unpacking the bag, which was full of sandwiches, cookies, fruit and the bottle of milk. "Dig in." she said, handing out the sandwiches. Emma thought to herself that the family's next good meal might not come until the next day when they arrived in Toronto; however the brochure that described the train trip indicated that a light meal was available to passengers. It consisted of sandwiches. Henry and Emma agreed that once in Toronto they would find a restaurant and have a good meal.

At eleven o'clock, the train started to move. It started rolling slowly through Halifax and didn't take long to clear the city limits. Before long, the huge locomotive picked up speed and steam could be seen flying past the windows. Soon, it was winding its way through the countryside. The landscape was so different with trees that they had never seen before. One of the other passengers pointed out different trees to them — pine trees, fir, balsam, poplar, hemlock, elm, oak and cedar trees. Not much could be seen of the foliage, which had fallen in autumn and so was covered in snow.

"Look at the rocks" Henry said in amazement. They were so big that the workmen building the railway had had to blast their way through. They were solid granite and they were huge. Before long, Roland spotted a deer, then another and another. It seemed like every ten minutes, Roland was yelling, "There's another one. Still, no moose though." But then it happened, just as the family was getting used to the scenery it happened!

"There's one! Oh my gosh, it's huge, A MOOSE." cried Roland.

They all looked in amazement. It was huge indeed, standing nine feet tall, with a rack of antlers that were at least six or seven feet wide. It was the most magnificent creature the family had ever seen. They stared at it as long as they could while the train sped by. Then it was gone. Roland sat down speechless. Both Emma and Winifred took out their sketchpads and began drawing what they had seen while it was still fresh in their minds. They had begun sketching images roughly since the beginning of the trip, but intended to complete them at a later date. Roland couldn't stop talking about the moose that they had just seen. Emma assured him that she would make an extra special effort when drawing his moose to make it look exactly as they had seen.

The train was travelling slower now for some reason. It had been clipping right along and Henry had thought to himself that, at this rate, they would complete the trip in record time. At this slower speed, though, it would take all of the three days they had been warned about. Henry would ask the conductor when he walked by. In the meantime, all their attention was focused outside the train. What a beautiful country this was, completely different from England. Everything here was big. The trees, the rocks, the animals and the weather were all harsher. The family had never seen snow like this. It was deep and even piled on the branches of the trees. They also were just noticing that the cold weather was freezing the moisture on the windows of the passenger car. Emma commented that just from what she had seen so far on their trip, she had enough subjects to draw for years.

Roland piped up and said, "Don't forget my moose, mom"

Emma assured him that his moose would be the first thing she would draw. Henry saw that the conductor was entering their car and waited for him to get close before putting his hand out.

"Yes sir, can I help you?" said the conductor.

"I was just wondering why the train had slowed down?" asked Henry.

"Well we have to reduce speed sometimes when the snow gets deep like this, otherwise there is the chance of derailment. The cold weather effects the tracks sometimes, both in winter and summer, actually summers are worse because the tracks actually warp when it gets too hot." replied the conductor.

"But not to worry sir," he went on. "We are on schedule. By the way, the dinner car is two cars ahead of this one, and supper is served starting at six o'clock." Other wise we provide sandwiches for free. The dinner is very reasonably priced and is well worth the cost.

"Oh that's great," replied Henry. "I was wondering about that. Thank you so much for the information."

The conductor turned to make his way to the back of the car, and when he opened the door to leave, a burst of very cold air flooded the car. As Henry sat enjoying the trip, he looked around the car to see what other people were on board. Of the fifteen or so passengers in this car, there was another family of four and two couples. The rest were a group of men possibly railway employees or workers of some kind.

Roland had asked permission to explore the train with Winifred. His mother told him that it would be nice to know what the dinner car was like, and so as long as they promised to be on their best behaviour they had permission. Emma seemed content to continue her sketches. Henry had acquired some literature at the train station in Halifax, so he took this opportunity to read it. The pamphlets were about Toronto and the Province of Ontario. However, it had been a long day and rising at such an early hour was having its effect on Henry. Before long, he hung his head down and fell fast asleep.

Emma decided to find the conductor to ask him about the sleeping arrangement for the night. Going towards the rear of the train, and entering the next car, she found that it was divided into two tier sleeping compartments. As she was inspecting the sleeping conditions, the conductor entered the car.

"So this is where we sleep?" asked Emma.

"That's right, Mrs. Bruce. Let me just check my list. Ah yes, here we are. Your family is in berth 22, down this way." the conductor said as he led her down the car stopping at berth 22.

"Here we are Mrs. Bruce. There are upper and lower berths — kids on top, I suppose." the conductor chuckled.

"It will have to be. I'm not climbing up there." Emma mused.

The berths were a little small, but looked comfortable enough, and a curtain could be drawn once one was inside making it private. Confident that there were proper sleeping accommodations, Emma returned to her seat in the passenger car. The children weren't there and Henry was still snoozing. It gave Emma quiet time to think about all the events that had transpired over the past few weeks. She wasn't very happy about leaving her home and all her friends, not to mention her family. As Emma was close to her mother, it had been hard telling her that they were not only moving away, but moving out of the country.

Emma had asked her parents if they would be interested in moving to Canada at a later date once Emma and Henry had established themselves in the new country. Her parents told her that although they doubted they would consider the move because of their age, they wouldn't say no just yet. Emma's mother understood why they were moving away and even said that regardless of the gang, it was time for Emma and Henry to strike out on their own and establish a new home for themselves. Emma said that living with Henry's father had always been a temporary arrangement. It was going to be different not having her parents close by for support. They had always been understanding and supportive toward Emma and her husband. The children would miss their grandparents as well who tended to spoil them a little too much; if that were possible. Emma thought to herself, *that's life isn't it*, and then chuckled when she thought of what her dad used to say "Chicken one day, feathers the next". Emma's dad was always saying weird things like that.

"Mum, Mum,"

"Ah, the kids are back. Yes Roland?" Emma queried.

"The conductor said he would take me up to the locomotive to meet the engineer, if it's ok with you and dad." Roland said barely able to contain himself.

"But we have to wait until the next station when the train stops." Roland continued.

"What about Winifred?" Emma asked.

"She doesn't want to see it." said Roland.

"Well that sounds exciting. I guess that would be okay, as long as you don't try driving." quipped Henry, who was now awake.

"Oh dad." moaned Roland.

The train was about an hour and a half out of Quebec City. According to the conductor, they would stop in Quebec City for an hour or so and then continue on overnight south to Toronto. As long as all went well, they would arrive in Toronto just after noon tomorrow. Meanwhile, it was almost dinnertime, which was to be served at six o'clock so the family had a half hour before they would make their way to the dining car. It had already got dark outside and the only light visible was the light being cast from inside the passenger car. Roland had told his parents that he had seen another moose, a small one this time with no antlers.

"That was a female moose. They are called cows. Males are called bulls, and only the males have antlers." said Henry. After that little lesson in moose biology, it was time to make their way to the dining car.

The family found seating together about half way down the dining car. Mom and dad were on one side of the aisle and Winifred and Roland on the other. All four meals were the same, roast beef with Yorkshire pudding, potatoes and gravy. All in all a very tasty meal, which the Bruces consumed with vigour. The family relaxed at their tables after dinner was finished. Emma and Henry talked while the kids stared out the window. Every now and then, Roland would point at a light in the distance and questioned his dad.

"Do people really live out there?" asked Roland.

"Sure, farmers or maybe hunters." replied Henry.

"Maybe Indians!" exclaimed Roland.

With their bellies full, it was time to head back and get settled in for the night.

The train was slowing down and more lights could be seen out of the window. They must be pulling in to Quebec City, Henry thought to himself.

"We seem to be coming into Quebec City, just in time too. You'll be able to see the locomotive before bedtime Roland." said Henry.

"Do you think the engineer will let me blow the whistle?" Roland asked excitedly.

"Maybe," replied Henry.

"Is it okay if I go and find the conductor?" asked Roland,

"Yes, go ahead, but be good." said Emma.

The Bruces minus Roland returned to their seats in the passenger car to relax a bit before retiring for the evening. Thirty minutes later, the Bruces were tired and each in their own little world, when the silence was broken by someone who had entered the passenger car and started calling out "Henry Bruce, is Henry Bruce here?" the man yelled.

"Over here." Henry called back.

The man identified himself as being from the telegraph company and said, "I have a wire for Mr. Bruce. Could you please sign here?"

"Of course." Henry said. He signed for the wire and was then handed an envelope.

Emma said "I wonder what that could be."

Henry opened the envelope and read the message contained inside.

TO: MR. HENRY BRUCE STOP
CARE OF THE CANADIAN PACIFIC RAILWAY STOP
THEY KNOW WHERE YOU WENT. STOP
NOT SURE IF ONE MAN FOLLOWED. STOP
WILL TRY TO FIND OUT STOP
BE CAREFUL. STOP
FROM: WILLIAM PERT, LONDON STOP

Henry was in shock. He handed the wire to Emma without saying a word. She read it and handed it back. He immediately placed the wire in his pant pocket.

"What was that mum?" Winifred asked

"Nothing dear, just a note from home." said Emma.

With perfect timing Roland entered the car and ran to his seat.

"You smell of smoke." said Winifred.

"You should see the locomotive, it's huge, and they let me shovel coal into the big furnace thing." Roland said excitedly.

"That was the boiler." said Henry.

Roland could sense that something was wrong. His mom and dad were too quiet when they would normally be asking all kinds of questions about what he had seen in the locomotive. He knew enough not to ask questions so he sat down. For the rest of the evening, the family sat in relative silence. About ten o'clock, Emma piped up and announced, "It is time to go to bed."

"Follow me to our huge bedrooms." Emma said jokingly.

With that, she got up and headed for the sleeper car, followed by the rest of the family.

"Here we are," arriving at bunk twenty- two.

"You guys are up top while your dad and I are down below." said Emma.

The family settled into their bunks for a well-deserved rest. Tomorrow, they would arrive in Toronto, right on time, unless something untoward happened.

When Emma and Henry retired for the evening, Henry whispered to Emma "Don't worry. I'll take care of everything."

It was an uneasy night for Emma, as she couldn't help worrying about all that had gone on. The noise and the motion of the train didn't help bring on a restful sleep at all. Emma couldn't even toss or turn because the bunks were so small. To make matters worse, Henry began to snore, which he did when he was overtired. Emma swore the whole train car would be kept awake by his snoring.

SIX
HAPPY NEW YEARS

Emma and Henry had been so preoccupied with the trip that they had lost track of the date. As it turned out, the day that they arrived in Toronto was New Year's Eve. In other words, they would usher in the New Year in their new country and new city.

Henry wondered if his uncle had received the letter that he had sent just before leaving London. He also wondered what the reception would be like when Henry and his family showed up at his uncle's front door. If for whatever reason the greeting was less than inviting; Henry and family would be forced to find lodging for the night. As well, Henry would be forced to find a job immediately, and then seek out a more permanent residence. After buying the clothing in Halifax and all the expenses paid out for the trip, Henry calculated that they had enough money to live on for the month of January. This did not include the portrait money made by Emma and Winifred on the Teutonic.

Before leaving London, Henry and his father, George, had had a lengthy discussion about what Henry could expect by moving to Toronto. At first, life would be difficult, even with his uncle Thomas' help. George told him not to expect to arrive in Toronto and be taken care of by Thomas. As soon as they got there, Henry would have to find his own way. His father said that life tended to be tougher over there. After all, it was a very new country — still very wild and unforgiving. Henry asked about his uncle Thomas as he wanted to know what type of man he was. Was he married? Did he have children? Thomas had kept in touch with George over the years since their parents had died, and since his move to Canada.

In his letters, Thomas would relate the story of his move to Canada, how hard it was to make a living and gain any kind of foothold in such a large and foreboding land. When he had landed in Halifax, the same way Henry had, he had very little idea of where he would go. He listened to other single men and heard what they had to say about their choices in where they would try to settle. Thomas had stayed in Halifax for a period of a month trying to decide what path he should follow. He really didn't want to become a farmer, not having any training in that vocation. He would rather try to continue tanning, which he had worked on as an apprentice back in London.

The big question was where to go. He had narrowed his choices down to three — Montreal or Toronto, which were the biggest cities in the eastern part of Canada, or Thomas thought he could just hop on the train and see where it took him. This would be the most daring choice, but in a land as big as Canada; one never knew what opportunities might become available. He would have the most promise for employment in Montreal or Toronto. Finally, he chose Toronto as his destination. From what he had heard and read, Toronto was a lot like London, having received many immigrants from the British Isles. Language would not be a problem as it might have been if he had chosen Montreal. Thomas did not speak French.

In his letters, Thomas indicated that he had been gainfully employed soon after reaching his chosen destination. It wasn't long afterward as well that he met Teresa, a lovely young Irish woman that he ended up marrying. Thomas had started working as a tanner's apprentice again, and, before long, had established himself in the trade. His wife, like Thomas, had no family in Canada as she had travelled from Ireland with two other young women. According to Thomas's letters, he and his wife were happy in their new life together in Canada.

The family awoke when the train came to a stop. All four got dressed in their bunks and then headed back to their seats. Along the way, they looked out of the train windows and discovered that they were stopped at a train station at a town called Kingston. Henry knew from the map he had obtained in Halifax that Kingston was a town on the shores of Lake Ontario and was about three hundred miles from Toronto. That meant that the train should reach Toronto by noon or one o'clock.

It was seven o'clock and time for a good breakfast, which would be their last meal they would have on the train. They made their way to the dining car to find their tables had been set for breakfast. Before long, they were eating, what they came to know as good Canadian bacon with eggs. Emma gave instructions to the children to pack all their belongings as soon as breakfast was finished in preparation for getting off the train. The conductor happened to walk by and stopped to talk to the Bruce family.

"So how did you like your visit to the locomotive, Roland" he asked,

"It was great. Thank you so much for taking me, sir." replied Roland.

"Yes that was very nice of you. Thank you." said Henry.

"My pleasure. Enjoy the rest of your trip. We will be in Toronto before you know it." said the conductor.

In London, there had been another murder in Whitechapel. The police were in a quandary as they thought the murders would have stopped after they had arrested '*Leather Gloves*', but he was in jail at the time of the murder. If '*Leather Gloves*' wasn't '*Jack the Ripper*', it meant more of the gruesome murders could be expected. Most of the gang had been released from custody with insufficient evidence to proceed to trial. Most of the prostitutes that were to have given evidence relating to the extortion charges had disappeared. The only good thing that had come of the raids in Whitechapel was that the gang had disbanded. So, more theories as to who '*Jack the Ripper*' was were starting to surface. At one point, they even thought that he was one of the royal family. Another theory was that he had fled the country possibly fleeing to Canada. Only time would tell.

So far, five murders had been attributed to the vicious killer, but in fact there were probably more murders that may have occurred before this set of homicides.

When they were settled, Henry fully intended to write to both his father and William Pert. He wanted more information from William about his wire that was so urgently sent and received while they were on the train. It had been a panic message warning Henry to be careful. He wondered who would have followed him and why. Was it just the money, or was it more sinister, maybe revenge. Henry had checked all the passengers on the train and had satisfied himself that there was no one from the gang on board. Once in Toronto he would start to take precautions.

Henry's thoughts turned to William Pert and what a good friend he had been. He truly hoped that William and his wife would make the trip to Canada. Nothing would be better than to go into business with William and possibly with his Uncle Thomas. Both Henry and William would be much younger than Thomas, by as much as twenty years. Henry wasn't sure if Thomas had his own business or worked for someone else. In any event he would be a skilled craftsman by now, which would raise numerous possibilities. Henry started to daydream about the future, owning his own shop with William, owning property and treating Emma and the children to the better things in life.

It was noon and as Henry had predicted, the train was coming into an area that seemed a lot more populated. The further along they went, the more houses appeared. Finally, the train was pulling into Toronto Station. According to the documents that Henry had acquired, the Toronto railway station was named Union Station and had been totally rebuilt reopening in 1886, three years prior to their arrival to serve the 180,000 people in Toronto. It was described as the main corridor for the Canadian Pacific Railway and joined the West of Canada to the East. As soon as the Bruce family exited the train, they realized that they were in a fully modern facility. The building itself was immense and made of more expensive building materials such as limestone, marble and granite. This was far nicer than any train station in London. Across the street from Union Station was the Queen's Hotel, which was also owned by the C.P.R.

The city itself was like a boomtown with construction going on everywhere. Henry thought to himself, *if we have to stay in a hotel tonight then it will be the Queen's Hotel for us.* Meanwhile, he had to find out how to get to Gladstone Avenue where Thomas lived. After a few inquiries, he learned that streetcars ran the length of Queen Street, which would take the family right to Gladstone Avenue. If Henry informed the driver of where he wanted to go; the driver would call out the street when they got there. Henry thought: *Oh my God, they even have streetcars!*

It was a short walk up to Queen Street, then a ten-minute wait for the streetcar. Once on board and seated, the family sat in awe of the city that they now found themselves in. The streetcar ran on electricity from wires strung overhead in the road. Apparently, Queen Street was one of the main streets that ran east and west. Gladstone Avenue was about five miles to the west and would take over thirty minutes to get there, which meant the family had thirty minutes of entertaining travel ahead of them. It was a chance to take in the sights. They passed hundreds of small shops and houses — all fairly new and very well kept. The driver finally announced to the Bruces that they would be at Gladstone in just a minute or two. Minutes later they were there.

"There you go folks, Gladstone Avenue, and that's the Gladstone Hotel right on the corner," said the driver.

After thanking the driver for his assistance, the family exited the streetcar and went to the sidewalk. "Ok." said Henry, "Now we are going to #26 Gladstone Avenue — should be just up the street a bit."

The day happened to be clear, but cold as the family walked up Gladstone Avenue carrying all their baggage.

"Well there it is." said Henry.

With great apprehension they went to the door. Henry hadn't seen his uncle for quite a long time and wasn't sure if Thomas would recognize him. He knocked on the door and waited. Before long, a gentleman answered the door, "Thomas?" said Henry

"Oh my gosh you're here. We had no idea when you were going to arrive." exclaimed Thomas.

"Teresa, come see who's here," Thomas yelled into the house.

Thomas shook Henry's hand and gave Emma a big hug. They introduced their children and then were led inside the house out of the cold. Teresa came from the back of the house and was just as excited as Thomas to see her new relatives.

"We have so much to talk about and guess what? You're here on New Year's Eve. I just can't believe it!" exclaimed Thomas.

After their coats had been taken and hung up, they all sat in the parlour. Not a big room, but it had six comfortable chairs and several small tables.

"You people must be cold, hungry and tired." said Thomas

"We can take care of all of that in short order… Right then tea first." said Teresa.

It was as if a load had been lifted off of Henry's shoulders. After all, it was because of him that the family had to move from their home in London to this new land. Emma was tired from the trip and was a little overwhelmed with all she had seen since landing in Halifax. Henry hadn't realized how hard it had been on her until she looked up at him and broke down crying.

"Now, now, dear. Everything will be all right. You're safe now, you're with family." said Teresa.

"I'm sorry. I'm just a little tired." said Emma.

Thomas entered with the tea so soon the travelers were having tea and cookies. The rest of the afternoon was spent catching up. Everyone had his or her own story to tell. Henry would tell his story to Thomas in private away from young ears.

"Tonight we dine on roast beef with baked potatoes and all the fixings. At some point, you people should catch a nap because we all must stay up to welcome in the New Year. I have also saved a nice bottle of wine for the occasion." said Thomas

"That sounds wonderful" Henry piped in.

Emma thought to herself that she would love to lie down for a while. She truly was tired from the trip and hadn't slept much on the train, so she would welcome an opportunity to catch a quick nap.

Henry and Thomas had decided to take a walk to the Gladstone Hotel to have a pint. They had a lot to talk about, but couldn't do it around the others. Thomas found it extremely interesting when Henry related the story of *'Jack the Ripper'*. Of course, Thomas had read all about the murders in the paper, but here was a family member that

Enigma In Whitechapel

had actually come from the very area where it was happening. Thomas knew the area well, but had lost touch with the friends that he had left behind when he came to Canada. He also knew of the gang that Henry was running from.

"You're a smart man coming here. I don't think they will chase you this far. They were active when I lived there and were trying to make a name for themselves." said Thomas.

"They're mean and vindictive. I wouldn't be surprised if they had something to do with all those murders in Whitechapel." replied Henry.

Thomas and Henry talked for well over an hour, discussing the past as well as the future. Henry told Thomas all about his friend William and how he had helped him escape London. Thomas felt sure that Henry would be able to find work as a tanner, and said he would help him as much as he could. As far as Henry starting a business of his own, Thomas felt that it was possible, but that it would take Henry years to become established enough to tackle an ambitious undertaking like that. The two men made their way back home and, as they opened the front door, were greeted with the smell of a roast beef dinner in the oven. The two men had developed an appetite during their talk. Emma and the children had rested while the men were gone and Teresa had attended to dinner. Emma had assured Teresa that they would help with all the chores of the house, while her family stayed there.

After dinner, they all gathered in the parlour for more good conversation while they waited for the ringing in of the New Year.

"We will know when the New Year arrives because the bells will ring at the local church a block or so away."

Teresa told the Bruces. She went on to add, "We have done the best we could as far as sleeping accommodations are concerned. A bedroom upstairs is able to fit four borrowed cots. You are welcome to stay here as long as it takes to get back on your feet and find more appropriate lodgings."

"Tomorrow is New Year's day which is a holiday. The stores will be closed, but what we could do is go for a long walk along Queen Street so that you can get familiarized with your new surroundings." said Thomas. He continued to tell them where their church was, and where Thomas worked. Thomas also knew where the schools were and could show them to the Bruces.

SEVEN
THE STRANGER

In Halifax, another ocean liner had arrived from Great Britain. As the passengers started to disembark, a noticeably large chap made his way down the boarding ramp. He seemed to be alone, and brushed by the other passengers pushing his way ahead of them. He was tall, standing 6'3" and was well built. Even though, he was wearing a heavy overcoat, his muscular physique could still be made out underneath. The strange passenger travelled light, having only one satchel as baggage. He entered the immigration building, and about an hour later could be seen leaving it and walking north with a determination of someone who knew exactly where he was going.

There was a knock at the door and when Mrs. Godfrey answered it, this large man was standing there.

"May I help you?" said Mrs. Godfrey.

"Hello, my name is Tony. I wonder may I ask you some questions about some people who may have stayed here?" he asked.

"Yes. It's cold. Please step in." said Mrs. Godfrey.

"Thank you. I was informed at the immigration office that recently a British family named 'Bruce' may have stayed here a few days ago." said Tony

"That's right. A lovely family they were. They were anxious to move on to Toronto to stay with family there." said a naïve Mrs. Godfrey.

"I wonder if you would have a room I could rent for this evening" Tony asked.

"Yes, just for one night Tony?" Mrs. Godfrey inquired.

"Just one night or until I can get the next train to Toronto. In the meantime, I have some errands to run. I'll be back later this evening. May I leave my bag here?" inquired Tony.

"Yes, of course." replied Mrs. Godfrey unknowingly admitting a possible murderer into her home.

With that Tony turned and exited the house. Mrs. Godfrey wondered too late what business this strange man would have with the Bruces. He really wasn't like the Bruces at all. He seemed secretive and his demeanour was far coarser and unpleasant compared to the Bruces. She thought to herself if she knew where the Bruces had gone in Toronto she could wire them.

Tony meanwhile had gone to the train station and booked passage on the next train bound for Toronto. He then walked back into town to try and buy some heavier, warmer clothing. To his disappointment, he found the stores were closed. As his train would not leave until noon the next day, it would give him time to find a store and buy whatever he needed before the train left. Meanwhile, he would find a restaurant and get a good meal under his belt.

In Toronto, the Bruce family enjoyed their day walking around and becoming familiar with the area. The children liked the school, as it was new — having been built no more than five years ago. It was a large building, well built with large windows. A large playground and soccer field were alongside it. Even an ice rink had been built next to the school, where hockey players were now skating back and forth. The Bruces had never seen skating before and so were amazed at how fast they could travel and how graceful they looked. Roland thought to himself that he wanted to try that out for sure.

Thomas had taken Henry to the shop where he worked and although they could not go inside; Thomas was able to point things out from the windows. Henry was very impressed and hoped that one day he would be working or even own a similar establishment. Henry thought to himself that, first thing in the morning, he would head out on his own to seek employment. It was imperative that he get a job, as he did not want to impose on his uncle Thomas, for any longer than he had to. Even though, Thomas and Teresa were the nicest of people; the Bruces wanted to be on their own. After all the time they had lived with Henry's dad, it was time they had their own residence. Already it was starting to get dark, so it was time to return home and prepare dinner. Emma helped in the kitchen, while Thomas and Henry discussed good employment possibilities for Henry to apply for. The children were tired and it wouldn't be long after dinner before they went to bed.

The train pulled out of Halifax on time. Tony had purchased a new coat and boots earlier in the morning and had got to the train station just in time. Twenty minutes later the train left the station. Before he left Mrs. Godfrey's rooming house, she had started to ask him questions about the kind of business he had with the Bruce family. When Tony was evasive with his answers, he could sense that Mrs. Godfrey was becoming suspicious so he changed the subject by complimenting her on her beautiful home.

In fact, Tony was right. Mrs. Godfrey had become suspicious so she had decided to try getting information from the immigration office. She might be able to talk to a friend of hers that worked there to see the destination the Bruces had put on their immigration forms. Mrs. Godfrey was able to get the address in Toronto where the Bruces had headed, and decided to send a wire from the telegraph office to alert Henry about this large stranger named Tony. The wire was sent just before closing and the operator made assurances that it would be delivered first thing in the morning.

Henry was up early and at Thomas' suggestion accompanied him to work. Thomas thought it wouldn't hurt to introduce Henry to his employer Mr. Jacques. Maybe he could suggest other shops to apply to. Emma would take the children to the school to see if they qualified for enrolment. Of course, Winifred and Roland were excited at the prospect of being enrolled in a new school in their new country. The Bruces knew that a good education almost always assured success in the future. None of the children they knew from back home were well educated, so they were more or less confined to a future of working on the docks.

The scenery outside the train window captivated Tony. He had never seen such beautiful landscapes. Everything was new to him. He saw an abundance of wildlife he had never seen before, and the trees and shrubs were amazing. He liked what he saw, even the snow as deep as it was mesmerized him. He was tired of the life he had been leading, as he didn't like being feared and labeled a thug and a gangster. He had done that type of work for far too long. He decided he was due for a change; maybe even settle down and where better than in Canada.

Jake the gang leader had given him orders. He was to follow Henry and his family, get the money Henry owed Jake, and then kill him. Tony began to hatch a plan. He would find Henry Bruce and get the money owed to Jake, but he would not harm Henry or his family. He would then keep the money and find land to buy for himself. He had always had thoughts of becoming a farmer. He loved hard work and could think of nothing better than to be out of doors all day. At thirty years of age, he had a lot of good years in him. His sexual tendencies were not a consideration, as the isolation of starting a new life, as a farmer would offset his sexual desires. Tony had the rest of his train trip to Toronto to make a final decision.

Mr. Jacques, Thomas's employer, had given Henry a list of places to check for a job. Henry had tried two of them with no luck, as they weren't hiring right now. Henry was on his way to a third location, but along the way happened on a leather shop just north of Queen Street. He thought he would go in and have a word with the owner. Henry explained he was looking for work and that he was an experienced tanner back home. The owner, Mr. Freeman was very impressed with him and said that he was planning on expanding his business, but had no available time to train anyone new. He thought maybe Henry would work out, as he was an experienced tanner. It looked like Henry had come by at a very opportune time.

Things were already looking up for the Bruce family. Henry returned home to Thomas' house with great news. Emma and Teresa were both home when Henry burst through the front door.

"What's wrong?" Emma screamed.

"I got a job. I got a job. I start work next Monday. What a great country!" Henry shouted out.

"Oh my God," Emma said enthusiastically.

The two danced around the kitchen like a couple of kids. Then Teresa joined in.

Henry finally sat down and told them all about his experiences of the day. He said that, although, it wasn't a great deal of money at first; he would receive a substantial raise in one year. The agreement Henry had struck with Mr. Freeman was that Henry would receive 17 shillings per week to start with and this would be raised after the first year. This would give Henry about 68 shillings a month to live on in the first year.

"Wait, where are the children?" Henry said with concern.

"Oh, with all the excitement, I forgot to tell you. They have been enrolled in school." said Emma.

"What a great country. We've been here less than a week, and look what we've accomplished." said Henry.

Henry couldn't wait for Thomas to get home from work to tell him the great news. This new turn of events meant that Henry and Emma could start looking for a place of their own to rent. He would have to talk with Thomas about how much it would cost per month to see if they could afford it. Until then, they could live with Thomas and Teresa rent free, but would share the expenses, such as food. Thomas returned home from work shortly after five o'clock. After hearing the good news, he insisted on taking Henry to the 'Gladstone' for a pint. The two men found their seats in the men's parlour and before long were sipping their first pint.

The men's room or parlour was a large room in most hotels or taverns that was restricted to men only. Another room next to the dining room was for ladies with escorts. Solo ladies were not permitted so women had to be accompanied by a gentleman.

Henry recounted the day's events to Thomas and thanked him for taking him to meet Mr. Jacques. He told Thomas it was a fluke of luck that led him to talk with Mr. Freeman, his new boss. Thomas told Henry that he had heard of Mr. Freeman and his shop and said that he had a reputation as being a little hardnosed, but he had a successful business. In all, Thomas felt Henry's deal with Mr. Freeman was adequate. He felt at some time in the future, Henry would be better off working for someone else. Henry agreed and said that, as long as the job paid the rent for the next couple of years, he could put up with Mr. Freeman.

After enjoying their second pint of ale, the two men returned home. Teresa approached Henry and handed him a wire that had come for him earlier in the day. Henry assumed the wire was from William Pert in London, but was shocked to read that it was from Mrs. Godfrey back in Halifax. Henry unfolded the wire and it read:

TO: MR. HENRY BRUCE
   26 GLADSTONE AVE., TOR., ONT.
   — MAN ASKING QUESTIONS ABOUT YOU   STOP
   — DIDN'T LIKE HIM   STOP
   — LEFT FOR TORONTO TODAY   STOP
   — BE AWARE   STOP
   — FROM: MRS. GODFREY
      HALIFAX NOVA SCOTIA

Henry looked at Emma with raised eyebrows. Emma knew not to ask questions as yet. She would wait until they were alone.

Roland and Winifred heard their father at the front door and came running, excited to tell their dad about their new school and to congratulate him on getting a job. After dinner, Emma and Henry went for a walk along Queen Street to discuss the contents of the wire.

"It looks like I may have to defend myself, love." said Henry.

"What do you mean?" asked Emma.

"I'm not going to let some thug ruin our new beginning. I thought about this after the last wire that we got on the train. I decided then that I would obtain a gun once we got here. I'll ask Thomas about getting one. Don't say anything to the children or Teresa, okay." explained Henry.

Emma expressed her concern, but really knew very little about handling a situation like this. She would have to rely on Henry's judgment. Henry assured her that all would be all right. He knew that if the stranger had left Halifax that afternoon, he wouldn't get to Toronto until tomorrow afternoon at the earliest. This gave Henry time to prepare.

Back in London, the police were in a quandary. They had no new information about 'Jack the Ripper', and their investigation was becoming frustrated. Numerous avenues of investigation had been looked into with negative results. Sir Melville McNaughton was determined to find the answers to the murders; his reputation depended on it. The murderer, first dubbed 'the Red Fiend', then 'the Whitechapel murderer' and then finally 'Jack the Ripper' was believed to be responsible for the murders of Mary Nichols, Annie Chapman and Elizabeth Stride all of who had had their throats slashed.

He was also blamed for the murders of Catherine Eddowes and Mary Kelly. These last two women were skinned to the bone and Catherine Eddowes had had her face mutilated. These five murders were in the same area and had other similarities in the way the murders had been carried out. Four more murders had also occurred after the initial five. These were of Alice McKenzie, Francis Coles, Emma smith and Martha Tabram. The last four murders although in the same area were not attributed to 'Jack the Ripper'. It was thought the police did this to keep the public from panicking and to ease the pressure on the police.

At the dockyards, Henry's bosses wondered what had happened to him. It wasn't like him not to show up for work. It wasn't that unusual for men to go missing, though. Some men were *'shanghaied'*, which happened when unscrupulous sea captains were short of crew. They would order their men to basically kidnap a longshoreman, or someone off the street, before setting sail. When the kidnapped man was out to sea, they would release him so he could work as a crewmember. Hundreds of men were *shanghaied* every year. Once out at sea, the men had no option, but to work. If they didn't; they ran the risk of beatings or being thrown overboard. The bosses would ask William Pert, who they knew was a friend of Henry's, if he knew anything. Failing that there was nothing else they could do.

Henry had five days before he started his new job. This gave him five days to deal with the stranger from Halifax. He would first send a letter to Mrs. Godfrey thanking her for her wire. He would tell her that the large stranger was just an old friend and that there was no need to be concerned. Henry would also have a talk with Thomas about obtaining a firearm. That night, before everyone retired for the evening, Henry had a talk with Thomas. He explained the problem he could be facing, and asked about the firearm. Thomas understood but seemed a little bit disgruntled about the situation. Reluctantly, he agreed to give Henry a six shot revolver that he had in the house, with the condition that Henry only use the gun as a last resort. Henry assured Thomas that he had no intention of using the gun unless he was forced to. In any event, he would not tell anyone where he got it. Henry would get up early and get the gun before Thomas left for work.

Henry had devised a plan to handle the stranger. Once he got the gun from Thomas, he would go back downtown by streetcar and make his way to the train station. There, he would check on the anticipated arrival time of the train from Halifax. As long as the train was still coming in on time, Henry would wait there to make sure he didn't miss the arrival of the stranger. He was sure he would recognize this person, if he was from the gang. He would then follow the person until they were alone in a secluded area and confront him. If the stranger was there to collect the money he owed; Henry would point the gun at him and tell him not to bother him again or else he would face the consequences. Hopefully, this tactic would deter the stranger, but at the first sign of trouble, Henry was prepared to use the gun.

Henry could see any trains pulling into the station from his vantage point across the street. When he saw the train come in, he thought that the stranger would appear walking out the front door about thirty minutes later. So the name of the game was to wait. Henry had time to think while standing there in the cold. If he could get his family past this series of unfortunate events; he felt sure that the future would hold promise for the Bruces. Henry's thoughts turned to William Pert, maybe he should have convinced him and his wife to travel to Toronto with them. For the first time in this long voyage, Henry felt very alone.

He was shocked back to reality as he saw a train pull into the station. It shouldn't be long now. Then, there he was. He was unmistakably 'Leather Gloves' or Tony" from London. He came out of the main entrance of Union station and walked across the street to the hotel. Henry thought maybe Tony was going to stay there the night, but Henry had to make sure. If Tony was going to stay there; then he could confront him in his hotel room. Henry eased himself around the corner and watched as the big man entered the hotel. Then, he waited for Tony to come back out. An hour passed. Just as Henry was about to go into the hotel to see where Tony had gone; he walked out the front door of the hotel and turned right walking west toward Henry's location.

Henry stayed back until Tony passed, then walked behind him. At the next street, Henry closed in until he was directly behind Tony. He pulled the gun from his pocket and walked up to Tony sticking the barrel in Tony's back and said

"Walk up this alley or I'll shoot."

The two men made their way up the street and into the alley. Henry let Tony turn around. As soon as he saw who his attacker was, Tony started to smile.

"Well blow me down. Look who it is." muttered Tony

"Yes it's me. I want you to leave me and my family alone." Henry said

"If you had paid Jake the fifty pounds you owe him; I wouldn't be here. You brought this on yourself." replied Tony

"Don't make me hurt you Tony. I'm not a violent man, but I won't let you harm me or my family." asserted Henry.

Just then, Tony lurched forward grabbing Henry by the arm that held the gun. The two men struggled violently until Tony was able to raise a fist and strike Henry on the jaw. Henry went down but didn't pass out.

Tony then grabbed the gun from Henry's hand and pointed it at him. Henry's life flashed before his eyes. He knew he was a goner. Then out of nowhere, Henry heard a thud and with that Tony's eyes rolled back in his head and he fell. Standing behind him was Henry's saviour.

"Oh, my God, Emma!" Henry yelled

Henry got to his feet, took the gun from Tony's now limp hand, and then turned to Emma. The two embraced each other. Emma was sobbing.

"How did you know?" asked Henry

"I knew you were going to try something to protect us. I couldn't let you go alone. I took the next streetcar after I saw you take the Queen streetcar. I knew you were going to the train station so if I took the next streetcar; you wouldn't see me. I got off one stop further and walked back. I waited until I saw you walking into the train station and then waited for you to come out. I thought that you were going to wait for this guy so I waited up the street where you couldn't see me. Then I followed you up the street and watched until he punched you. Then I used this iron bar to give him a clout on the head." said Emma smiling proudly.

"You've saved my life, love." said Henry.

Henry turned and looked at Tony, who was still lying on the ground out cold. Now, what do we do with him? Henry wondered.

"We could shoot him and tell the police that he tried to rob us" said Emma.

"Let's try talking to him. Maybe we can bribe him." said Henry

Tony started to moan, and then sat himself upright obviously in a stupor.

"What the hell happened?" moaned Tony

"I told you not to try to harm us. You didn't think I came alone to meet you did you?" inquired Henry.

Tony shook his head and then sat quietly for a moment.

"I got knocked about before I had a chance to talk to you. I was sent over here by Jake to get his money and then kill you." he said.

"I expected as much, but I really didn't think you would come so soon" said Henry.

"I wanted to tell you what has happened back home. Please believe me when I tell you that you have nothing to fear from me." said Tony.

"Have I got your word you won't try and harm us." said Henry.

"As long as your wife promises not to bash my head again..." Tony quipped.

Henry helped the big man to his feet, and then suggested they go to a nearby park where they could sit down and talk in private.

EIGHT
AN UNEASY PEACE

Tony bent down and scooped up some snow to put on his now aching head, while the three walked to a nearby park. They picked a secluded park bench in a corner of the park. Tony plunked himself down, while Henry sat at the other end of the bench with his hand clutching the gun in his pocket. Emma stood next to Henry, still with her pipe weapon in hand.

"What did you have to tell us?" said Henry

"Well it's a very long story, but I really must tell someone before it drives me to my grave." said Tony. He leaned back, took a deep breath and then related the following story: "First let me say again that I mean you no harm. I have to tell you the whole story so you completely understand. I was born in London not far from Whitechapel. As a child, other children as well as adults always ridiculed me because I was always very large for my age. In fact, I was as strong as a twenty-year-old man when I was fifteen. This caused me so many problems, especially, with other boys. I liked being around — older men. Eventually that led to me being 'a molly' (gay). Because of my size I could beat up anyone no matter how big they were.

I started hanging around with gang boys, who needed muscle. I fit the bill exactly. If any of them brought up my being 'a molly', I would beat them to within an inch of their life and think nothing of it. The gang boys all had women that they would pass around. All those women were deathly afraid of me so had nothing to do with me. As a matter of fact, the bitches would accuse me of doing things to them, just to see if the men cared for them. I guess they were trying to make them jealous. I started to hate them. Most of them were prostitutes, which made me hate them even more.

I was a full member of the gang right from the beginning and did most of their dirty work. When someone defaulted on a loan, I was the one who went to collect, and if they didn't have the money, I made them pay in other ways. I'm not proud of all the things I did, but that's life. I won't lie to you. I've broken legs, arms and, yes, I've killed people.

When Jake told me he was having problems collecting from his girls working for him in the Whitechapel area, he asked me to go down and straighten them out. I started hanging around Whitechapel and when I saw one of them, I would take them aside and remind them of the rules. Sometimes they would try to argue with me, which led to my reminding them in a very painful way to abide by the rules or else — with that, I would break something, a finger, an arm, a hand or whatever. Most of the girls got the message and the money started flowing again to the gang, which pleased Jake. Jake was afraid of me. I think I was the only man he was ever afraid of. I told him once I would work for him and do most anything he wanted, but if he ever talked behind my back, I'd break every bone in his body.

Things were going along fine until the girls working Whitechapel started causing problems again. Jake was furious. He told me they had to make an example of one of them. That night, I went down to Whitechapel and found Mary Nichols. When she argued with me, I put my knife to her. I hated the bitch anyway. She always tried to make fun of me. I enjoyed killing her." Tony stopped and looked at Emma, then at Henry. Both were in shock, but said nothing. Tony continued with his story.

"Jake was pleased with my work, but was still having problems with these women. He wanted more done to teach them a real lesson. I went back to Whitechapel, and before long saw another one of the girls. Her name was Annie Chapman. I followed her late in the night and when I caught up to her, I put my knife to her like I did with Mary Nichols. When I went back to see Jake, he told me that everyone was talking about the murders in Whitechapel and that I should get out of sight for a while."

"Are you telling us that you are 'Jack the Ripper'?" asked Henry in disbelief.

"Yes and no. Let me continue." insisted Tony. He then continued with his story. "I had a talk with Jake and told him that if I kept doing this; I would probably get caught. Already rumours were going around that I was the Ripper. Jake agreed and just said to leave it with him. Over the next week or so two more women were murdered down near Whitechapel — Mary Kelly and Catherine Eddowes. When I heard about the murders, it bothered me. Not that they got murdered, but the fact that they were mutilated. Catherine had her nose cut off and I think their breasts were severed off as well. I told Jake I wouldn't have any more to do with his mutilations. He understood and said that he had two other men doing his jobs for him. I didn't ask any more questions.

It wasn't long after that that we got word that you had left London for Halifax. Before we could do anything, the Bobbies were at our doors and arrested all of us. I was questioned for hours about the murders, but kept to my story that I knew nothing about them. Then they just released me. I had felt confident that I would spend the rest of my days in a prison.

I had to hunt down Jake. The gang had been dispersed. When I found him, he told me that he was going to get everyone back together, but it would take time. He had a job for me, though. He wanted me to hunt you down, get his money back and then kill you. I told him that I would, so he gave me five pounds for my expenses and said to contact him when I got back. Within days, I was on an ocean liner headed for Halifax although I had no idea where you had gone from Halifax.

I had a cabin in second class, quite nice it was. It was private and quiet. I had a lot of time to think about my situation as a whole. A lot of things started going through my head. Although, I had relations with older men; I still had urges where women were concerned. I was and still am very confused about myself. I thought that the only way to discover who I really am was to start anew. These thoughts haunted me the entire ocean trip. When I got to

Halifax, I learned from the landlady, Mrs. Godfrey, where you had gone."

"You didn't harm her did you?" Emma blurted out.

"No, of course not. She was a nice woman and treated me well." answered Tony.

He continued with his story. "I made a decision to finally decide what to do with my future while on the train. My choices were fairly simple. I could kill you after getting the money back for Jake, go back and return it to him, or I could get some of the money you owed Jake and use it to help me buy a farm and start fresh here. If I chose the latter; I know Jake would send someone to deal with both you and me. So, I made my decision. I'm staying here to start a new life. I've decided to look for a wife as well. I want to leave my old ways behind. I want to replace violence with hard work, and I want a family. That is my story, I hope you believe me, it's the truth."

Emma and Henry looked at each other in a bewildered way. Should they believe Tony and trust him or should they just try to get rid of him.

"You put us in a very bad spot, Tony. To trust you would put our lives at risk, if you are lying to us." said Henry.

"We only have a small amount of the money left, but we need it to get ourselves started in our new life." said Emma.

"I have enough money to live on," said Tony, "just not enough to buy a farm. I had planned to take a room near you, and spend my time learning how to buy the farm. I also need to make contacts here, you know with people who own farms. Maybe I'll get a job as a farm hand, but whatever I do, I want to stay close to you two until we know what Jake's reaction will be. I have people who will be writing me to keep me updated. They will warn me when they learn of troubling news that I must be made aware of." Tony said.

"Ok, Tony, it sounds like you really have thought this through, but we will be watching you too. If you go back to breaking the law here; we will have to protect ourselves. How much money are you expecting from us?" Henry asked.

"Why don't we just wait and see. Over the years, I too saved a bit of money. It might even be enough to get me the farm. I have no idea what they are worth." said Tony.

This was an unexpected turn of events, to be sure. Tony seemed sincere in his story. Henry realized that he could never totally trust him as the result could be catastrophic. So, he decided that if Emma and he were going to go along with Tony's story; it would require Henry carrying the gun on him at all times, just in case. It would also mean that he would have to write Mrs. Godfrey so she could warn them if any other travellers started asking questions about them or Tony. Henry would also write William Pert and ask him to keep his ear to the ground as it were, to also warn them if he heard anything about Jake, and the gang.

"Where do we go from here, Tony" asked Henry.

"Well, I still need to find myself some living quarters, and settle in, I will always keep you apprised of my plans. Should I hear anything from over home, then I will deal with it." said Tony.

"Ok, Tony, it's a deal then. We will help you if you help us." Henry said

"Fine then, Henry. It's a deal" said Tony.

The two men then shook hands.

Emma and Henry left Tony in the park. Tony was still putting snow on his head from the blow that Emma had inflicted on him. They made their way to the streetcar stop and waited for the next car. The streetcar ride home was a quiet one with neither Henry nor Emma saying much at all. Emma went to lie down until the kids came home from school, while Henry set to writing his friend William. It would be a rather long letter. There was so much to tell him. The most important request was for William to watch the goings on of the gang and to report any unusual behaviour to Henry as soon as it happened.

In the letter, Henry told William of his new job and how the kids had been enrolled in school free of any fees or tuition. He also told him that, although the situation with Tony had been handled, he still had a very uneasy feeling about the whole situation. He would feel much better if William was in Toronto watching his back. Henry had never wanted to harm Tony, and with this new turn of events Henry felt cautious about the future. Henry wondered, though, if a leopard can change its spots. Tony was a cold-blooded killer. He had showed no remorse for his victims, but did feel sorry for himself. Henry thought time would tell, but, in the meantime, he would be on his guard at all times.

In London, the police were trying to find Tony, as there were more questions that he needed to answer. Jake was the only one who knew the identity of the murderous pair of men that he had sent down to the Whitechapel area to deal with his prostitutes. They were very dangerous and Jake didn't like dealing with them. He had told the two assassins to ease up on the ladies of the evening, but really wasn't sure what they were doing or how many women they had butchered. It was possible that in their lust for murder they were now acting independently. The police had been to Jake's door looking for Tony, but Jake had just told them that he hadn't seen Tony since he got out of jail, but of course he neglected to tell them he had sent Tony on a special assignment.

The next morning, after Thomas had left for work and the kids had gone to school, Emma and Henry decided to check the newspaper for nearby houses that were for rent. They had decided that as soon as Henry started being paid at his new job, it would be time to move into their own residence. That, of course, was dependent on the affordability of the new lodgings. Thomas had told Henry that he had a few articles of furniture that he could have, which were currently being stored in their basement, and he could take the borrowed cots until they got their own. Then, they would have to be returned to their owners.

While looking through the newspaper for houses, Henry noticed the advertisements for the sale of land. It appeared that one hundred acres of prime farmland in a good location could cost as much as six hundred and fifty to seven hundred dollars Canadian. These prices were at the top end of the scale. Cheaper farms could be had for a lot less, but required more work as the land needed to be cleared of forest or rock. Henry also saw advertisements for farms in remote locations that cost no more than five hundred dollars.

At that time, one-pound sterling was equal to approximately four dollars and forty cents in Canadian money. Henry decided to save these adverts and give them to Tony the next time he saw him. As for a house to rent, Emma and Henry would take a day and go to inspect a few in the area. It would take a month for Henry to make enough money for the necessary deposit in order to rent a unit, without using the remaining money that they had brought with them from the old country. They had agreed to put that money aside in case of emergency.

The children were now settling in at school. Apparently, Emma had done a good job in her home schooling attempts back in England. Winifred and Roland found that they were not behind in their knowledge base at all. This would make their studies much easier as they went along. Winifred had been placed in a grade eight class while Roland was placed in a grade six class. As they were so new to their respective classes, it would take a while for them to get to know any of the other children.

Tony had decided to take a room at The Queens Hotel opposite the train station. While he was checking into the hotel, he saw a small group of men standing at the front counter. They seemed to be arguing with the desk clerk about their rowdiness the previous night. The men started to become more belligerent and yell at the clerk. The manager of the hotel then tried to intervene, which caused the men to become even more uncooperative to the point of threatening the desk clerk and the manager. Tony felt he should step in and offer his assistance to the manager and clerk.

"What's the problem here?" Tony growled

"Mind your own business, mate." one of the men fired back.

With that, Tony grabbed the man by the throat and lifted him in the air. One of the other men tried to come to his friend's aid, only to be punched in the mouth as Tony knocked him to the ground.

"You men behave yourselves so you'll be able to walk out of here under your own power. If you don't, they will have to carry you out understand?" demanded Tony.

"Yes sir," the three men said in unison.

As luck would have it, the manager of the Hotel approached Tony after he had checked in and engaged him in conversation. The manager, a Mr. St. Pierre, told Tony that he was in need of a head of security for the hotel. Tony's size and physical attributes impressed the manager, as well, as how he had handled the disorderly men at the front counter. At times such as now, unruly travelers from the trains from out west descended on the hotel and caused trouble. These men could be cowboys, railway workers or men who had been trying their luck gold mining. Mr. St. Pierre needed someone bigger and meaner than these adventurers.

Tony straight away advised the manager that he would be interested in the job for one year, and would let him know at that time, if he would stay on. Mr. St. Pierre stated what the wages would be and said that he would also give Tony one of the best rooms in the hotel and all his meals at the restaurant. This sealed the deal as far as Tony was concerned. Not only would he be earning money that he could save, but he was across from the railway station. If any of the men from back home came to town, they would head to the hotel to stay and eat. Tony could deal with them legally at that point. By then, though, he hoped to have got to know the local constabulary and gain their trust.

Finally, Tony could leave the life of being a thug behind him. He would have to remember to go easy, though, on the people he would be dealing with here as they would be good hard working men — not thugs and their women would not be prostitutes. He would have to treat them fairly, but firmly when correcting their errant behaviour. Tony was invited by the manager to move in right away so he could start work any time he wanted. Tony replied that he would do that… it seemed that he had already started work.

Although the wages were modest, the fact that room and board came with the agreement made the deal very profitable for Tony. Thankfully, Mr. St. Pierre had not asked for any references from him, or where he had previously worked. The fact that Tony was in need of a job was good enough for the manager.

NINE
A NEW LIFE

Six months had gone by and the Bruce family had accomplished so much. The two children were doing very well indeed at school. Both had made it to the top of their respective classes by the end of the school year and had graduated to the next level. Winifred had captured the hearts of her teachers by becoming a prolific artist, the best in the school. Meanwhile, Roland had excelled in sports and had showed an interest in his science and math studies.

A couple of the boys who thought they could bully Roland learned the hard way that he was not to be tangled with. He had proved that he was tougher than any of them. He would not put up with any form of bullying of himself or any of his friends. In fact, his friends snickered at the bullies that there was a new sheriff in town!

Emma and Henry had searched for months to find a house that they could rent and set up as their new home. Thomas had assured them that they were not imposing and that they were welcome to stay with them as long as they wanted. Henry could tell, though, that their presence in the Bruce household was in fact a great imposition so, after a couple of months, he felt that it was time to move on and be on their own. The house they rented was not that far away on Brock Street, about one mile from Thomas's house. Thomas and Teresa helped the family move into their new residence. Teresa was, especially, good at interior decoration, which was of great assistance to Emma. Thomas went around doing handy man jobs of affixing nails and screws to put things on the walls.

The new house had three big bedrooms, a large kitchen and parlour as well as a large front porch where Emma and Henry could sit during nice sunny days. A railway line was about half a mile from the house so at night, they could hear the sound of the locomotive whistles going off as the trains sped by. The family was very happy with their new home.

Henry had started work at the Tannery and was doing very well for himself. The expansion of the business had gone quite well. Henry was making a real name for himself with management and customers alike. It would seem that people in this new country had a different attitude toward work than that at the docks in London. Over home, if you didn't work as hard as you possibly could, you would lose your job, because too many other men without work were willing to do the job and work twice as hard. In Toronto, the work attitude was more laid back. Good tradesmen were few and far between. If you were good at your job, as Henry was; you could work at your own pace. Henry was used to getting the jobs done quickly and efficiently, which pleased the owner to no end. In fact, the pay raise promised at the end of the year came early at just six months.

Emma too had secured a job in a bookstore, stacking the shelves and attending to customers. She took to the job straight away. As an added bonus, she was able to show some of her artwork for sale, with a ten percent fee to the owner of the shop. Emma set up a sort of studio in the rear porch area of their new house.

At first, she was drawing in pencil, mostly landscapes that she and Winifred had witnessed on their train trip to Toronto. After doing seven or eight of these sketches, she decided to try her hand at oil painting and had great success in this endeavour. All of the paints, brushes, canvas and other items she needed were all paid for from her wages at the bookstore.

Henry had received a letter from his friend, William Pert, who had expressed his shock in finding that Tony had followed Henry and family to Toronto. After only six months of being absent from the area, his name rarely came up. Every now and then, William heard that Jake was still looking for Tony, but nothing would ever come of it. In the letter, William also told Henry that he felt bad that he was not in Toronto helping his friend. William went on to say that he and Sarah had been saving their money to move to Toronto in the near future. He also added that about two months after Henry had fled to Toronto, the murders in Whitechapel had stopped. The police had made no arrests, but there were plenty of rumours circulating as to who the 'Ripper' was. The police apparently had ruled out Tony, as a suspect because one more murder had occurred after Tony had disappeared. That last murder had been the most brutal of all.

Henry was pleased to hear from his friend and so decided to write him back in short order, to keep him up to date with all that was going on. Henry also would express his concern about not having seen Tony again since the incident at the park. Henry felt this was very odd. Tony had promised to keep him apprised of his situation. Now, it had been the better part of six months and Henry had heard nothing from the man. In his letter, he would tell William that he planned to take a trip in town to try to find out what was going on with Tony. Henry, also worried about his aging father, would also ask William to check on him. Henry and Emma had even thought of paying for George's passage to Toronto to stay with them in the new house. It was futile to write George a letter as the old man could not read or write. In the letter, he would also ask William to suggest that George come to Canada as well to be with them. If he agreed, then Emma and Henry would send money and make the arrangements. He thought it might even be a better idea to have George live with his brother, Thomas. All of the possibilities could be discussed, if George decided to make the trip. The bigger question was when William would be able to make the move. Henry would assure William that he would have a place to live and a good probability of a job in the shop where Henry worked.

Henry was perplexed with the situation concerning Tony. He just had to find out what he was up to — things were too quiet. It was Friday afternoon and Henry was not required to work the following day, which would give him ample time to journey downtown to try to find Tony. First thing the next morning, he was up and out the door headed for downtown Toronto. Henry had the letter to William Pert ready to be mailed so before boarding the streetcar, he mailed it at the corner post box. While on the streetcar, Henry's thoughts turned to where he would possibly find Tony, and where he would begin his search. He thought that the train station might be the first place to enquire, then the hotel across the street. Failing that, he would check the hospital. Maybe the crack on the head that Tony had received from Emma's pipe was a little more serious than they had thought. Then, he would check with local restaurants around the train station to see if they produced any information. First things first, the check at the train station.

Henry had asked Emma to draw a sketch of what Tony looked like. She had drawn a very good likeness of him so that anyone who had seen him would surely recognize him from the sketch. When Henry asked the cashier at the station if he had seen such a man, he immediately replied, "Of course, mate, that's Tony."

"Do you know where I can find him, sir?" asked Henry

"He works right across the street (pointing to the hotel)," replied the cashier.

"Might I ask how you know him, sir?" inquired Henry

"Sure, he's the hotel's head of security — the Hotel detective you might say. Thank goodness, he came our way, my friend. We've had very little trouble with the rowdy ones since he showed up — not like we used to have." explained the cashier.

"Thank you for your help, sir" replied Henry.

Well, that explained a lot, Henry thought to himself. He chuckled that the bugger had got himself a job doing what he does best — busting heads. Henry decided to pay Detective Tony Drummond a little visit. As he approached the front desk of the hotel, he saw Tony out of the corner of his eye, standing near the manager's office. About the same time, Tony saw him and started over toward him.

"Hello, Henry." Tony barked.

"Well, well, if it isn't Tony Drummond. How are you mate?" said Henry

"I'm very well, and you and the family?" asked Tony.

"Very well, thank you. Say, is there anywhere we can sit and get caught up?" asked Henry.

Tony motioned for Henry to follow him. They entered the men's room of the hotel where Tony told the bar tender to bring two pints over to his table. The two men made their way to a table in the corner of the back of the room.

"So what's going on?" Henry asked

"Well, after I left you and Emma that day, you know — when she cracked me on the head, I came in here and helped the manager out a little." replied Tony.

He then told Henry the whole story of how he had got the job and how he really liked working there. "I like it so much that I am going to give up the idea of being a farmer. This is the type of work I have been born to do. ..."

Henry had to agree with him that he had special talents when it came to keeping the peace.

The two men talked for well over an hour and became friendly with one another. Tony gave Henry the impression that he was not the man he used to be. Tony also related how he had been accepted by the Toronto Police and had actually been made a special detective by them; even though, he had no powers of arrest other than those that every citizen has. He was sworn in by the local magistrate to keep the peace while in the employ of the hotel. The police had already brought him in on several cases pertaining to the hotel, which he had gladly assisted on. He had used his citizen's powers of arrest on no less than ten occasions, holding the culprits until a constable could take over.

Tony then asked Henry if he could trust him not to say anything about Tony's previous life; as if it ever got around, he would be forced to leave. Henry assured the big man that he would say nothing and that his secret was safe. Tony went on to say that he was also aware of inquiries that had been made about him in Halifax by two men from the old country. "If they ever show up here, I'll deal with them; if you know what I mean." asserted Tony.

"I understand," said Henry

On the way home, Henry had a lot to think about. He was pleased that Tony had found his niche in life on the right side of the law. He also wondered who the two men were who had been making inquiries about Tony. If they had been sent by Jake back in London, who would they be after more Tony or himself? With Henry, Jake was just trying to collect a debt. With Tony, Jake's concern was his treachery after Tony had disappeared without saying a word. Would Jake assume that Tony had collected the money from Henry and then went his own separate way? In any event, Henry decided to meet with Tony every other week or so to keep up to date and avoid trouble. At the least Tony could be reached at the hotel any time day or night.

TEN
THE BROTHERS

Henry arrived home to find a note had been pinned to the front door. Henry took it. Thinking it was from Emma, he went into the house to read it. At first, he thought Emma had gone out shopping so had left the note. Soon, he realized it wasn't from Emma at all. It was from Thomas, who was concerned, as he had seen two black men snooping around his house for the past couple of days. They would walk by the house on Gladstone straining to look inside, then walk over to the hotel where they stayed for several hours. Then, they would walk by the house again, and then disappear. If it had happened just the once, Thomas said, he wouldn't have been concerned, but after the second time, Thomas felt there was more to it than met the eye.

After reading and rereading the note, Henry decided to pay Thomas a visit to make sure he was all right. The walk took but fifteen minutes at a brisk pace. Before long, Henry was knocking on the front door at 26 Gladstone Ave. Thomas answered and ushered Henry inside rather hastily.

"They're in the hotel now. Have you any idea who they are?" said Thomas.

"No, but I hope they're not from over home," Henry replied.

"I just got back from talking with Tony Drummond, who said he had had word that two men had been asking about him in Halifax, a few days ago." admitted Henry.

"Do you think that Jake sent them from London?" asked Thomas.

"I don't know, but it's possible. Look you must be careful, Thomas. Whatever you do, don't let them in the house. If you have to summon the police, do so. They could have been sent here by Jake, which means they will be very dangerous men. I'm going to have to go back downtown and tell Tony about this. Maybe he can handle it for us." Henry said.

Henry left the house by the back door. Then, he followed a laneway out onto Queen Street, a block away from Gladstone Ave. He boarded the next streetcar heading Eastbound for the short trip to the hotel. Once there, he located Tony who was standing near the front desk. After Henry had related what had transpired, the two men agreed that Tony should return to Gladstone with Henry. With any luck at all, the two black men would still be in the Gladstone Hotel when they arrived. Tony advised the front desk clerk that he had to be gone for several hours and then left with Henry.

As the streetcar pulled up in front of the Gladstone Hotel, Tony recognized the two men standing out front as Everton and Livingston Magumba. They were two brothers from the gang that Tony had seen with Jake back home. Jake had never introduced them, but Tony had heard through other members of the gang that they were very odd fellows indeed as they practiced witchcraft, voodoo and all sorts of mumbo jumbo that Tony frankly had never heard of before. Both brothers were in their thirties and of average height and build. According to other gang members, Jake would call them in when he had special jobs that he needed done. Without doubt, they were ruthless killers.

The Magumba brothers had indeed been sent to go after Tony and Henry as vicious debt collectors. They were very strange men and had a story of their own to tell, which Tony had heard from people in the gang. As young men, just sixteen and eighteen years old, they had lived with their family in Africa. They were very poor people and most of the time the land that they depended on for food was suffering from drought conditions. As the families in the village normally had a lot of children, it became hard for them to feed them. Many babies and young children died during times of drought. As a result, the families were large as they anticipated the deaths of most of the children. However, if the children were lucky enough to survive, their parents could not afford to feed them. They would often trade their older boys to men from Europe, who would give them blankets in return for the older boys.

This had been the fate of the Magumba boys. They had been taken from their village, but soon realized that they were nothing more than slaves for the white Europeans. They were taken aboard a boat bound for the Caribbean where they would be sold to slave traders for a handsome price. The slave traders would then resell them to plantation owners who made them work on their sugar cane farms. Many of these boys died during the trip to the Caribbean as the Europeans were ruthless with them. The two Magumba boys spent the next ten years as slaves, working in the fields. They were whipped almost daily and had scars on their backs to prove it. Occasionally, they would be sold to a neighbouring farm, but always seemed able to stay together. The slave ships would come to their island at least once or twice a year to sell the plantation owner more slaves and to replace the ones that had died through disease or over work.

The brothers, along with other slaves, devised a plan to take over one of these slave ships and then sail it to England. Several of the slaves had sailing experience so would be able to handle sailing the big ships all the way to England. The slave owners and their people would have to be killed to give the men enough time to make good their escape by sea. The day came for the uprising. The slaves who participated were lucky that the sailors and farm hands were hung over from a wild drunken party they had had the night before. The slaves took their machetes and used them to slaughter the whites on the farm. They made good their escape using the slave ship and headed straight for England. The plan was to run the ship aground on English shores and then head inland after they split up.

Livingston and Everton walked away from the coast, avoiding the farms and small towns along the way. The others had told the brothers that London would be the best place to hide because so many people lived there. So the two men would blend in with the black population already living there. This is exactly what happened, and before long, they had gained a reputation of being bloodthirsty savages. That's what drew the attention of Jake who hired them to do his dirty work for him.

They had been sent to Toronto now, but unfortunately, for them, Tony was about to recognize them.

"You let me handle this Henry." said Tony

Pointing to a store front, Henry said, "I'll wait over there just to see if you need any help."

Tony and Henry split up as they exited the streetcar. As soon as the two men saw Tony, they started to run. Tony chased after them, followed by Henry. They ran along Queen Street and then into a laneway.

Tony stopped running as this was the perfect setup for the two men. They would jump him as soon as he entered the laneway, but he was wise to tricks like that. Sure enough, as soon as Tony rounded the corner entering the laneway, one of the brothers tried to jump him. Tony saw he had a knife in his hand, which he grabbed causing a small cut to the palm of the other man's hand. Then, he levelled a merciless blow to the black man rendering him unconscious so that he dropped and lay limp on the ground. The other brother then confronted Tony, also with a knife in his hand.

"Drop the knife or I'll stick it in your bloody throat! DROP IT NOW!" yelled Tony.

With that, the man dropped the knife. He had heard of Tony and how mean he could be, he started pleading for his life and that of his brother.

"Please sir, don't kill us. We meant you no harm." said Livingston Magumba.

Tony became enraged. He knew exactly why the two men had travelled all the way from London. They had murder on their minds — no doubt about it. Henry turned the corner of the laneway and saw what was going on.

"What do we do now, Tony?" Henry enquired

"**We** do nothing. You leave these two to me. I'll take care of them." replied Tony.

"Go on get out of here!" yelled Tony

Henry had never seen Tony like this. He was furious as he grabbed Livingston Magumba by the throat. Henry walked calmly back to Queen Street and then to Thomas's house, who was waiting for him wanting to know what was going on.

Once inside the house, Henry told Thomas the whole story, and told him where he had left Tony with the two strangers.

"I've never seen Tony like that. He was so enraged, furious almost out of control. He was so mad" said Henry.

"What do you think will happen now?" asked Thomas

"I don't know. I told you what Tony did for a living before he came here to Toronto. He can be merciless when he wants to be. I wouldn't put anything past him at this point." replied Henry.

Back in the laneway, Tony took out a pair of handcuffs that had been given to him by his friends at the police department. He threw them at Livingstone and told him to handcuff himself to his brother. Still pleading for his life, Livingstone did as he was told. Everton, the other brother, was just starting to come back to consciousness, so Tony ordered him to stand up.

"You know what men, if you had of told me the truth about why you were here, I would have respected you. I'm no fool. Jake sent you here for the same reason he sent me here. To get his money back and then kill the lot of us." said Tony.

"No, no sir. We were just told to get his money back, that's all." said Livingston.

With that Tony, became enraged again. He started hitting the two men with his huge fists. He was brutal in the ferocity of his attack. Both men were beaten to the point that they had several broken bones. Tony kept up the assault until he became out of breath some five minutes after. When he stopped, the two men lay unconscious on the ground, bleeding, but alive.

Tony took the handcuffs off one of the brothers, reconnecting the handcuff to a nearby pipe. He then dragged the other beaten man further down the laneway to the site of an abandoned well behind a garage. Tony knew that the well was no longer in use as Toronto was on a citywide water system. Wells were no longer used. Tony picked the black man up and broke his neck with one quick twisting motion then threw him down the well. Tony then returned to the site of the fight leaving the one brother in the well to die. When he got back, it was only to find his handcuffs lying on the ground still connected to the pipe and Everton Magumba gone. He searched the area high and low with no result. Tony would have to check the local hospital later, but right now he had to return to work.

He thought to himself that he had busted Everton up pretty good so it would take a long time for him to fully recover from what had happened to him. With that, Tony got back on the streetcar and returned to the hotel where he acted as if nothing had happened. Henry returned to Thomas's house and told Thomas what had happened.

"I think the best thing for us to do if anyone asks, is to act as if we know nothing. I don't know what Tony did to those two men but judging from how angry he was, I sure wouldn't want to be them." said Henry. "I'm going home. I'll talk to you later, if you hear anything, let me know." as he walked out the front door.

That night, after the kids had gone to bed and Henry and Emma had retired for the night, Henry felt that Emma should be brought up to date with the events of the day. The two talked in whispered tones for what seemed to be an hour. Emma expressed her concerns and then started to cry. Henry consoled her and tried to reassure her. He was always a sucker when it came to Emma. She was so beautiful. When he felt that she was in a vulnerable mood, he couldn't help but hold her tight and touch her. As the two embraced and touched, it wasn't long before they were making passionate love.

A week went by, with no news from Tony. Henry would have to take another trip to the hotel to see what was going on. Meanwhile, on a more pleasant note, the family had received a letter from William Pert. He was writing to let Henry know that he, Sarah and Roger were planning on making the move to Toronto as soon as he heard back from Henry. He asked in the letter if they could stay with them until they found suitable accommodations. William estimated it would take them almost three weeks to get to Toronto. William went on to say that he had asked Henry's father if he was interested in relocating with them to Toronto. To which, his reply had been that he was too old to make the move. He would be fine where he was as long as he had the rent from the two extra boarders that he had allowed into his home.

Henry wrote back to William right away to assure him the family would be more than welcome to stay with them upon their arrival. Henry also thought it would be wise to tell William about what had been happening in Toronto between the black brothers and Tony. Henry told him how he was looking forward to having a friend close by that he could rely on in case the brothers came back. Henry also informed him of the rooming house run by Mrs. Godfrey in Halifax and suggested it would be a good place to stay until the train left for Toronto. If they were able to telegraph when they knew when their train was scheduled to leave Halifax; Henry could meet them at the train station in Toronto.

Henry then decided to take the trip to the hotel to talk with Tony. This would also give Henry the chance to mail his return letter to William. The next day was Saturday so as he was not required at work, first thing, in the morning he boarded the streetcar for downtown Toronto. Before long, Henry was walking in the main entrance of the hotel. He couldn't see Tony so was forced to ask for him at the front desk. The clerk told Henry that he hadn't seen Tony in a few days, but that was not unusual, as the clerk was just returning from his regular days off. The clerk gave Henry Tony's room number. Henry found the room and knocked on the door, but no answer. Henry then decided to sit in the lounge by the front desk on the off chance Tony had just gone out for breakfast. Henry waited for two hours, but Tony did not show up. Henry was becoming more concerned, which he expressed to the clerk at the front desk.

The manager of the hotel was summoned and the problem explained. He agreed it was unusual behaviour on Tony's part so they decided they should enter Tony's room. Armed with the passkey, the manager and Henry opened the door to Tony's room. As soon as the door was opened, a stench from inside hit the two men. Obviously, something had happened to Tony. The door was open just wide enough to allow the two men to see Tony lying on the bed. His throat had been cut and blood covered the bedding. The manager turned and rushed down the hallway telling Henry to stand guard at the door while he went to summon the police.

Henry was beside himself. His imagination went wild. His first thought was that the two black brothers were responsible. They must have got away from Tony after the incident in the laneway. Henry was unaware that one of them was actually dead, murdered by Tony. Then Henry thought what if someone else had possibly murdered Tony — someone that he had dealings with there at the hotel. In any event, that would be the job of the police to figure out. It was inevitable that Henry would be interviewed by the police, what would he tell them, what could he tell them. The police showed up on mass and locked the hotel down tight. No one could leave or enter until they had an idea about what had transpired. Henry was told to wait in the front lobby lounge until it was his turn to be interviewed.

Before long, a police wagon pulled up out front and two men with a folding canvas stretcher entered the hotel making their way to Tony's room. A short time later, they went out the front door with Tony obviously now in the stretcher covered with a sheet. Bloodstains had seeped through the sheet where his head was. The interviews started with the hotel clerk and then the manager; it would seem they were saving Henry for last.

Finally, an hour later, a detective came to get Henry. He led him to the manager's office where the detective asked him to empty his pockets out on the desk. After checking the contents of his pockets, the detective frisked Henry and wanted to see both sides of his hands.

"What's this for?" asked Henry

"We are searching for possible evidence, please have a seat." said the detective and motioned him to a chair.

Over the next two hours, Henry was interrogated over and over again by the lead investigator who had identified himself as Inspector Booth of the Toronto Police Homicide Squad.

Henry had prepared himself to tell the detectives the whole story leaving nothing out. This was the only way; Henry could distance himself from Tony's murder. Inspector Booth's Squad was a sort of an all in one unit. Although, they investigated homicides, and situations of suspicious death; they also investigated missing persons, which took up the bulk of their time. Homicides rarely occurred in Toronto. During the interrogation, Henry, of course, told the inspector about the two black men, and how Tony had beaten them both to within an inch of their lives. The inspector wanted the exact location where this had happened, Henry agreed to take the police to the laneway. Henry told the inspector that he couldn't believe the brothers had been able to murder Tony, not only because of Tony's size and his talent at fighting, but also because the two brothers had been so badly beaten.

As the intense interrogation went forward, Henry started his story at the beginning back in London, how he went into debt with the gang and that Tony was in fact one of its enforcers. He went on to tell the inspector of the plans he had made to get away from the gang and the letter he had sent to Sir Melville McNaughton just prior to leaving with his family. Henry also told him how the police in London were without many clues in the deaths of the prostitutes of Whitechapel. Henry had thrown them a false flag by implicating the gang.

The inspector listened intently interrupting Henry only occasionally to clarify part of his story. Henry further told him about Tony Drummond's following him and his family all the way to Toronto, as it had been his original intent to get the money back and then murder Henry. However, Henry also related how surprised he and Emma were when Tony told them of his change of heart.

The inspector then wanted to know who the two black men were, and their names. Henry could only remember their first names Everton and Livingston. He told the inspector that they too had been sent from London to get Jake's money and kill Tony, then do the same to Henry and his family. Henry said that Tony had only seen them a few times, but knew that they were very dangerous men. They had murdered and mutilated several of the prostitutes back in Whitechapel in London. They together might even be the figure known as 'Jack the Ripper', but Jake Skinner was the one actually behind the murders of the prostitutes.

Henry told the inspector that when he had read the note left by his uncle Thomas on his front door, he had been shocked. He went on to tell him that when after he met with Tony and were on their way back to confront the two strangers, Tony had told him that he would take care of the two men one way or another. True to his word, Tony had beaten them rather badly. That's when Tony told Henry to get out of there and not come back. The inspector interrupted again wanting Henry to take the police to the laneway, which Henry readily agreed to do.

At the end of the questioning, the inspector told Henry that the only thing he was guilty of was not informing the police of his problem when he had first arrived in Toronto. Technically, Emma was guilty of assaulting Tony, but because Tony was dead there was no case. Besides in the situation they found themselves in, with all the extenuating circumstances a conviction of Emma or Henry would not be possible. Inspector Booth told Henry that they would take him back to Queen Street near Gladstone Avenue. Henry could then trace the steps back to where he last saw Tony. A Police carriage was waiting in front of the hotel for the inspector and Henry. There was also a Paddy wagon with several police constables waiting to accompany the carriage. Before long, the carriage stopped in front of the Gladstone Hotel where the inspector and Henry disembarked from the carriage, followed by the police officers.

They soon located the laneway and Henry showed the inspector where the two men had been lying on the ground after the beating Tony had inflicted on them. The inspector observed some definite signs of a scuffle and also saw some drag marks, as if one of the men had been dragged further on down the laneway. This led to the rear of a garage and, as soon as they rounded the corner of the garage, they could smell a stench seemingly coming from the abandoned well beside the garage.

Henry thought to himself that it was the same smell he had noticed back at Tony's hotel room. The inspector asked Henry to stand back away from the well and ordered one of the constables to make sure nobody else entered the laneway. Other officers were given orders and immediately hurried to carry them out. The scene was now a crime scene, Henry overheard. Henry could see Thomas at the entrance of the laneway, so asked the officer watching him if he could speak with his uncle. He wanted him to contact Emma, his wife, to let her know he was alright. The officer agreed and Thomas was quickly updated as to what had happened.

Hours passed, while the police gathered evidence. There was indeed a body at the bottom of the well. It took considerable effort to bring it up without destroying valuable clues. Once the body had been brought up, and placed on a stretcher in the back of a police wagon, the inspector asked Henry to come and look at it to see if he knew the person. When Henry looked at the man who had been beaten badly, he could still recognize the man known to him as Livingston.

The inspector told Henry that he was very concerned that the other man Everton was nowhere to be found. He was going to have his officers do a thorough search of the area. The inspector advised Henry that he was free to go. He did want to place a guard on Henry's house in case Everton showed up with revenge on his mind. It looked to the inspector that Everton had murdered Tony and probably wanted Henry dead as well. The inspector would take out a warrant for the man known as Everton and alert all the officers in the area. The inspector told Henry before he left the scene that he would be around in a few days to talk more with him and to update him. Henry thanked the inspector and then made his way home. It had been a very long trying day and Henry just wanted to get home and pour himself a stiff drink while he related all that had happened to Emma.

ELEVEN
A DEATHLY CALM

Over two weeks had gone by, and the Inspector had been to the house several times with updates on the Tony Drummond murder case. The man found in the well had been positively identified as Livingston Magumba. The police in London knew him and his brother Everton. The inspector had informed Halifax Police to be on the alert for Everton Magumba, in case, he should try to make his way back to London. In the meantime, the Inspector had been trying to notify a next of kin for Tony. While searching Tony's belongings, they found a letter in his wallet addressed as "TO WHOM IT MAY CONCERN". The letter had the following note in it and was signed 'Tony Drummond'.

My name is Tony Drummond and I currently reside at the Queen's Hotel in Toronto Canada where I am employed as the Hotel Detective. Should anything happen to me, be it death or dismemberment, I hereby deem Mr. Henry Bruce of Brock Street, Toronto Canada, as my lawful next of kin. All of my property including my money is to be given to him. With that, Inspector Booth handed

Henry a manila envelope containing the personal effects of Tony Drummond.

Just after the inspector left the house, a wire arrived for Henry from William Pert advising that he and the family had arrived in Halifax. Their train would arrive in Toronto in two days. This would give Henry enough time to prepare a room for the Pert family. Emma was thrilled with the news and couldn't wait to see her friends. After discussing it, both Emma and Henry decided to take Friday off work to allow them to meet their friends at the train station. A nice meal would also have to be planned for Friday evening.

There would be no time to check the train station to see when the Pert's train would arrive in Toronto so Emma and Henry would go to the station after their kids had left for school. Henry thought to himself that because of their luggage and the fact that the Perts would be exhausted from the trip, that it would be a good idea to hire a cabbie for the trip back to Brock Street. They might even take the new arrivals on a site seeing tour around Toronto by the horse drawn cab. It would be a nice welcome for the new family upon their arrival. Therefore, right after Roland and Winifred left for school, Emma and Henry made their way down to the streetcar and then once downtown walked down to the train station. Henry checked with the clerk at the ticket cage to find out the estimated time of arrival for the inbound train from Halifax. The train was due in at about two o'clock baring anything unforeseen.

It was only ten o'clock, so the Bruces had four hours to wait until the train arrived. They decided to go for breakfast at a local restaurant and then Henry wanted to drop into the Hotel across the street where Tony had been murdered. He wanted to talk to the manager to see if the police had made any more headway in their investigation. After breakfast, the couple split up. Henry went to the Queens Hotel and Emma went back to the train station. She had no desire to be where Tony Drummond had been murdered.

It wasn't long before Henry was sitting in the men's beverage room in the hotel discussing Tony. The manager had no idea what Tony had done for a living prior to coming to Toronto. Henry filled him in on all the details, but for what it was worth he assured the manager that Tony had changed after coming to Toronto. After all, Tony was sent here to kill Henry and his family. Mr. St. Pierre agreed that Tony didn't seem to be a threat to anyone unless someone caused him grief. Mr. St Pierre had told him that a black man named Magumba was the one probably responsible for Tony's murder. He had read in the paper that a black man had been found dead in the west end. The manager wondered if the murdered man was involved in Tony's demise. Henry told him that there had been two brothers involved and that the murdered man in the West end was one of them, which left Tony's murderer still at large.

Henry returned to the train station around one o'clock and joined Emma who was sitting in the lounge waiting area. Emma tried to fill Henry in on all of the interesting people she had been watching, while she was waiting for him to return. One young couple waiting for the train must have been newly weds.

"Oh I remember being like that. When we were constantly whispering in each other's ear… the hugs, the little kisses, constantly touching or brushing up against one another."

"Mmmmm those were the days… right dear" said Emma. She looked over at Henry and could have sworn he was starting to nod off.

The ticket clerk announced in a loud voice that the train from Halifax was pulling into the station and the passengers would be arriving shortly. This was great news and right on time too. Before long, there they were William, Sarah and little Roger. They had three large travel bags on a dolly, which William was pushing. Emma and Henry ran over to greet them at which time hugs and kisses were exchanged.

Henry piped up to say, "We have a surprise for you. We are going to take a horse drawn carriage around town and then to our home. We know you're tired after your long trip so we won't be too long getting home. Your room is all ready for you and we have a nice meal planned for dinner." Emma said. William whispered to Henry that he was anxious for an update on all the news that had transpired since he had received Henry's last letter. William knew nothing of Tony Drummond's murder and the appearance of the two black men, one now dead and the other the suspected murderer of Tony. Henry planned to take William to the Gladstone Hotel and have a long talk with him. Meanwhile, the two families could enjoy a laid back afternoon looking at the Toronto tourist sites.

Before too long, the carriage pulled up in front of the new Bruce homestead. Roland and Winifred were just getting home from school and had been excited all day to see William and Sarah again not to mention little Roger.

Once inside and all their luggage put in their room, the two families settled down for refreshments. Sarah was in need for a good cup of tea, and then to lie down for a while. Roger was excited to see Roland and Winifred again, especially, Winifred who loved to spoil him because he was just so adorable.

Henry and William excused themselves and told the ladies they would be back in an hour or so. Emma understood while Sarah was a left a little confused thinking it was odd that they wanted to go to a hotel so soon after their arrival. Once outside, Henry started by telling William there was an awful lot that he needed to be told. First, he updated William on the quasi friendship he and Tony had fallen into after Tony got his job at the hotel. Then, there was the news that two black men, named Magumba, who Tony had known back in London had arrived in Toronto. Henry's uncle Thomas had seen them hanging around his house. Henry told William that he had rushed to the Queen's Hotel where Tony was to find him and tell him.

Then he outlined to William how, after filling Tony in on what was going on, the two men rode the streetcar back to Gladstone. On their arrival, they saw the two black men coming out of the Gladstone Hotel. Tony had chased the two men into a laneway and overpowered them. Then Henry told William what had happened in the laneway until Tony had ordered him to get out of there. Henry said how he had left Tony there, and gone to Thomas's house before returning home.

"What happened to the two black men?" inquired William.

Henry went on to tell him that as he had heard nothing from Tony for a couple of weeks, he had decided to go to see if he was all right. He then told William how he waited in the lobby area of the hotel for Tony, but became concerned. Along with the hotel manager, Henry went to Tony's room and found his body.

"Oh my God," exclaimed William.

Henry continued his story. "After I had given my statement to the inspector, he wanted me to take him to the laneway where Tony had beaten the two black men. After a short search of the lane, they found one of the brothers dead. He had been thrown down an abandoned well. There was no sign of the other brother...."

"Unbelievable!" said William.

"So as it stands now, they believe that sometime after his brother was murdered by Tony, he went back and murdered Tony." Henry said.

"How could one man kill Tony?" William asked.

"His throat was cut, but I don't know if that's what killed him. There's more bad news!" said Henry.

"What's that?" inquired William.

"The second brother hasn't been apprehended as yet!" stated Henry. "So, you have come at a good time. We must be on our guard in case this Everton Magumba shows up again. However, I am in possession of a handgun, which I keep in one of the upper cupboards in the kitchen. I will show you where it is when we get back home. If Magumba shows up; then William you can protect yourself."

Back at the Bruce house, the kids were outside playing with Roger. This gave Emma a chance to tell Sarah about the trouble that had befallen them. Sarah listened and then said, "It's a good thing we are here to help out." The two discussed the situation at length and agreed to keep a sharp watch out while at home. Sarah went to lie down while Emma started the evening meal. Before long, the two men were walking in the door. As the kids were outside playing and Sarah was lying down, Henry took the opportunity to show William where the gun was hidden. He also refreshed Emma's mind as to the location of the gun. William joked with Emma saying

"What are you cooking darling?"

Emma quipped back, "Cod's tongues and beans."

"Looks good, Emma. I like my cod tongues well done," said William giggling.

When dinner was over, Henry suggested they all go for a nice long walk to wear off the corned beef and cabbage dinner they had just feasted on.

"When we get back from the walk we can have our apple pie and cheese" said Emma.

Henry had told William that if they went for a walk, they could go down to Queen Street and pass the laneway where Tony had dispensed of Livingston Magumba. There was no need to mention it to the ladies and definitely not to the children. While near Queen Street, they could also drop in and say hello to Thomas and Teresa.

While on the walk, Henry discussed with William what he would like to do for a job. He told him, "If you are interested in being a tanner, I have already talked with my boss Mr. Freeman. As he expanded his business, he told me that if you work as hard as I do, he would be willing to hire you as my assistant."

To William, this was great news so he was ecstatic. If he could work with Henry; he would learn the trade more efficiently. The other benefit was that Henry would also be able to monitor the way William was learning the trade and help him get up to speed faster. All this, of course, was with a view of owning their own shop one day. The two men were great friends and would probably work well together. William could accompany Henry into work in a few days after he had rested and apply to Mr. Freeman for the job.

Sarah had told Emma that she would be stay at home all day taking care of Roger. So she would do all the laundry and cooking while Emma and the men were at work. Emma agreed to this saying that she would not take anything for rent in that case. As Sarah would be at home, Emma instructed her to be cautious of anyone loitering around the house. Emma had sketched a drawing of Everton Magumba so Sarah would be able to recognize him immediately if he ever showed up. The sketch was done with the assistance of Henry who guided Emma in drawing it.

TWELVE
THE DEATH OF TONY

When Tony had beaten Everton and Livingston in the laneway, Everton had been unconscious when Tony dragged his brother away. He had no idea that Tony was going to murder Livingston and, when he came to, he thought the best thing for him to do was to get away from the laneway and recuperate a little before trying to help Livingston. Everton had made it to his feet and then staggered out of the laneway. He was able to make it to the streetcar stop and board the next streetcar. He only travelled several stops, but felt he was far enough away that Tony wouldn't be able to find him. After getting off the streetcar, Everton was able to find a park bench and sit down. It would not take him long to feel better, he could then go back and relocate his brother. Had he known that his brother would be dead within minutes of being dragged away, he would have made a desperate attempt to help him.

Tony, in the meantime, had taken care of Livingston and went back looking for Everton. When he saw he was gone, he searched the immediate area, but, of course, Everton was already three or four blocks away. Tony walked around the neighbourhood, but time was running out for him. He had to get back to work. He abandoned his search and decided to get on the next streetcar to go back to the hotel.

Later, that day, Everton went back to the laneway to try to locate his brother. He thought that Livingston would be lying somewhere in need of help. Once at the laneway, Everton searched high and low for him until he heard a moaning coming from behind a garage. He followed the noise and before long had located his brother. Everton slid down into the well to be with his brother. His neck was broken and his breathing was very shallow and getting worse. It was obvious to Everton that his brother would not live through the night, so he stayed with him. He tried talking to him, but before long, even the moaning stopped. Livingston died in his brother's arms. Everton was livid. He swore revenge for his brother. He would make Tony and Henry both pay for what Tony had done to his brother. Everton stayed with his brother for the rest of the night, consumed with hatred for Tony and Henry.

The next morning, Everton climbed out of the well and after brushing himself off, boarded the streetcar heading downtown. He got off a few blocks before the hotel so as not to be seen by anyone who might recognize him. He then made his way to the back of the hotel and found a way to enter without being seen by any staff. Once inside, he made his way to the laundry room where he was able to steal some clothing to replace his own that had got torn and very dirty in the well. He also searched the office for any indication as to where Tony's room was.

Luckily, he was able to find a ledger, which contained washing instructions for the permanent residents of the hotel. He found Tony was in room 202 on the second floor. There was even a passkey hanging on a hook, which he took. He made his way via the back stairs, to the second floor. After finding Tony's room, he went back to the stairway to wait for him. At that point, Everton didn't know where Tony was so he had to make sure that he had the element of surprise on his side in order to take care of Tony. He waited and watched. People came and went, but no Tony.

Finally, Tony was there walking to his room. Everton's plan was to wait until Tony left his room and returned downstairs, then he would enter the room using the passkey, and wait for Tony's return. Tony returned to his room, finally, at noon. It was one o'clock, when Tony exited his room and went downstairs. Everton seized the moment and entered his room. Now, the advantage was on his side. Everton looked around the room for a weapon to hit Tony with. To his surprise, he found a nice metal bar about two feet long, just perfect for bashing Tony over the head with. Everton also had a hunter's knife with a ten-inch blade ready and waiting to slice into Tony's throat. Now, it was again just a matter of waiting for Tony.

It was already dark outside and Everton had to fight to stay awake, but it wouldn't be long now. His hatred kept him alert. Suddenly, Everton could hear the sound of a key turning in the door lock. The lights were out and Everton was waiting in the dark. Tony entered the room and, once the door had closed behind him, Everton hit him on the back of the head with the iron bar. Tony went down hard.

He was unconscious for sure. Everton lit an oil lamp at the bedside, which gave him just enough light to do what he had come to do. He pulled out the knife and with one sweeping motion slit Tony's throat from ear to ear just like he had done with the prostitutes back in London.

Tony's eyes opened wide and when he realized what was happening he tried to yell. All that happened was blood spewed from his mouth. Everton took his knife and cut off Tony's right ear, then forced Tony's mouth open and severed Tony's tongue cutting most of it off. Finally, Everton removed the thumbs of both hands. All of these body parts he put in a cloth bag, which he had with him. Later he would go to where his brother had been buried and place all of these body parts in the grave with his brother. This was an old African revenge ritual.

When an enemy warrior murdered another off the field of battle, the murdered warrior's family would seek revenge by killing the murderer and removing several body parts. An ear and tongue off were to keep lies from being told about the family member in the hereafter. As well, the murderer's thumbs severed prevented him from being able to hunt in the hereafter. When Everton found Henry, he would do the same thing to him. Everton stood over Tony and said "This is for my dead brother… Back home, I would eat your heart."

With that said, Everton turned and fled the hotel room. He walked back to the rear stairway and made his way out of the building. He would find some place to hole up until he had a chance to complete the second part of his revenge for the killing of his brother. Henry would be his next victim.

Early on a Monday morning, three days after William and his family arrived in Toronto, he and Henry made their way to Mr. Freeman's shop. Henry had discussed the matter of William's employment again with Mr. Freeman who told Henry he was looking forward to meeting him. William had his meeting with Mr. Freeman and agreed to his offer of employment. As William was not a journeyman like Henry, Mr. Freeman could only offer him an apprentice's wage, but assured him he would review this in six months. This was more than enough for the Pert family to live on, especially, if they could stay living with Henry. Better still, the job started right away.

William and Sarah began settling into life in Toronto quite nicely. William started work with Henry, and Sarah was enjoying her days in the Bruce house when everyone was away at school or work. She liked taking care of the two families and found the work easy and rewarding. She was a very good cook and always prepared dishes native to their London home, which the families really enjoyed. Occasionally, she would take Roger for a nice long walk down to visit Thomas and Teresa. Teresa would join them for a walk along Queen Street.

When Henry and William got home one evening, there was a letter waiting for Henry postmarked London England. Henry thought it would be a note from his father, George. He opened the letter and started to read. Before long, Henry's eyes welled up and he became visibly upset. He put the letter down and then said, "Dad died two weeks ago." He then went upstairs to his bedroom for some privacy. When Emma came home from work, she went up to console Henry. After a short time, they came back downstairs. Henry told everyone that the letter had been from his brother, Jack, stating that his father had become sick with the fever and slowly deteriorated. George had only sent for Jack when he knew he wasn't going to get any better.

George had made a will some years ago, leaving everything to his three children equally. In the letter, Jack told Henry that by the time Henry received his letter, George would have already been buried. Therefore, there was no real reason for Henry to come back to London right away. As far as his inheritance, Jack could wire the money to Henry's bank. It wasn't a lot of money, but it would still come in handy, if Henry started his own shop with William. As far as George's personal belongings, Jack and Madeline would keep them until Henry and Emma returned to London. If they didn't come back; Jack could forward a list of the property and Henry could choose a third of it that he might want.

The news of George's death came as a shock to Henry as he had mostly fond memories of his father. When he had left London for Canada, the thought had crossed his mind that he might never see his father again. Somehow, in the back of his mind, though, he believed that he would see him again before he died. He had continued to hope that George would come to Canada to live with him and Emma.

Henry had taken only two trips with him to The Tower of London where he had worked. The first construction of the Tower was in 1080 by William the Conqueror. Wild animals had been kept as in a zoo, on the property adjacent to the Tower castle until about 1830. George had taken his children to see where the animals had been kept and shown them around the grounds. Henry had liked it when his Dad also took them to see Tower Hill, where most of the executions had taken place. Henry and Emma had taken Roland and Winifred to the Tower many times, as they were interested in the Tower's extensive history, which went back hundreds of years. The kids had found all this history fascinating.

Jack and Madeline, Henry's brother and sister, had buried their father in the same cemetery as George's beloved Elizabeth their mother was buried. It was the very cemetery where all the other Bruce's had been buried for centuries — the St. Dunstan and all Saints Church Cemetery. George had requested this in his Will and Testament. Henry tried to imagine the funeral. From working at the Tower, George had a lot of friends that he had made over the years, as well as from St. Dunstan's Church where he had attended services all of his life. When Elizabeth was alive, they used to be quite active in the church, volunteering there whenever they could. With all these friends that they had made over the years, Henry surmised that his father's funeral would have been well attended.

***

In Tony's hotel room, Everton had stolen his money and added it to the money that the two brothers had been paid to do Jake's dirty work. This would be enough money to let Everton hide for a while. He knew the police had become involved and had found his brother's body. He had also overheard some men talking about how terrible it was. Now, Everton would wait. He rented a cheap room downtown and planned to stay there out of sight, for at least a month, only venturing out to buy food.

On several occasions, Inspector Booth dropped by to see if Henry had seen or heard anything about Everton Magumba. Henry had been constantly looking over his shoulder since Tony Drummond's murder. The inspector told Henry the cause of Tony's death was exsanguination, which is the draining of the blood from the body due to a severed artery or vein. In other words, Tony bled out. The inspector went on to say there were other cuts to the body, to his chest and abdomen. He also told him about the severed ear, tongue and thumbs that had been taken from the body at the time of the murder. He went on to say that this Everton fellow was a very brutal killer. The Inspector even ventured further to ask Henry if he thought that Everton could be 'Jack the Ripper'....

Henry admitted that he knew the Magumba brothers had been responsible for a couple of murders over the years in the UK and that two of them had been prostitutes in the Whitechapel area of London. Inspector Booth did say that it would be dangerous to assume that the brothers had committed all the Whitechapel murders or that these murders might be connected. However, he did admit it was suspicious and that anything was possible.

The inspector did tell Henry that Toronto had never had two such gruesome murders back to back and that he was lucky as he had all the answers for his superiors. He also assured Henry that when they did catch Everton Magumba, he would swing for his murderous ways. Before he left, the Inspector told Henry that he had ordered his men in the area to constantly check on the Bruce house while they were patrolling on their bicycles. He said,

"Trust me, when I say a black man will be very noticeable in this area."

On several occasions, Henry and William took their boys fishing. This was always an all day outing starting very early in the morning and getting home late in the evening. After numerous inquiries, Henry was able to learn the location of an excellent fishing spot. The Humber River, located about five or six miles to the West of where they lived, had plenty of fish, mostly trout and salmon. The men would bring home the catch of the day, which provided food for the table. What they couldn't use, they would give to Thomas and Teresa. Roland and Roger loved fishing mainly because it was a good day out with their fathers.

Meanwhile, Winifred and Emma would paint or draw on the days that the men were off fishing. Both women had honed their artistic skills and were starting to gain a reputation in the area mainly due to the bookstore. Emma was trying to become proficient at doing portraits as it was more lucrative than doing landscapes and still life. Winifred was concentrating on her landscapes. Sarah had taken up knitting and had produced several sweaters for the boys in advance of the upcoming cold winter.

Some days, Henry and William would take a streetcar ride to downtown Toronto and just walk around the main streets. They were looking for any sign of Everton Magumba. They asked questions about lodgings and restaurants, and on several occasions people had reported seeing such a man, but couldn't remember where they had seen him. There was no doubt in Henry's mind that Everton was still there somewhere, just waiting to strike. Henry felt certain that Everton believed that he had been in on the murder of his brother so only had revenge on his mind. This meant that no one was safe while Everton remained a free man. As a result, Henry got into the habit of placing a string of sleigh bells on the front and back doors of the house before going to bed. He also slept with the gun under his pillow. In his mind, these were acts of precaution not paranoia.

Everton, in the meantime, was running out of money. He had heard that some very wealthy people lived in certain areas of the city. He, therefore, developed a plan to rob several of them to get money to live on. With that in mind, he started watching two particular houses. Each one had just two people living in them. He had done his homework by finding out that these people were wealthy and owned their own businesses. One was a jeweller and the other a banker.

After a week of watching the first house, one day when the owners were both out, Everton broke in through a rear door. Once inside, he took his time searching the home. It was a large opulent building so it took Everton several hours to do a thorough job. However, he struck it rich. In the master bedroom, he found the lady's jewellery — thousands of dollars of diamonds and gold. In the upstairs office, he found cash after tearing the room apart. He found at least a few hundred Canadian dollars hidden under a loose floorboard. What luck! He was so pleased with his haul that he left the house, again by the back door. He had planned to stay in the home until the couple returned, thinking they would have a lot of cash on them. Rather than take the added chance, though, he left feeling satisfied with the goods and cash he had stolen.

After a few weeks, Everton was having a hard time converting his diamonds and gold into usable cash. The money he had taken was lasting, but he knew sooner or later it would run out. Before winter struck, he wanted to be on a boat headed for London. That meant he had several more months in Toronto. He would have to steal more money to provide a roof over his head. He started watching the second house that he had picked out earlier. It became obvious that it might prove to be a little harder target than the first home. Only two of people lived there, but they seemed to be more active. They came and went at unpredictable hours. No matter how long he watched them, he couldn't really plan a 'best time' to pull the job. What he felt reasonably sure of was that when they went out, they didn't usually return for at least several hours.

Once again, Everton entered stealthily through the rear door. He thought to himself that with any luck, he could quickly find some cash and leave. He started to search the house looking for an office. He didn't like dealing with jewellery so he disregarded the bedroom. He was able to find an office on the main floor of the huge home. After ransacking the office, he only found a small amount of cash. He started searching other rooms and eventually went upstairs.

He was becoming frustrated and stubborn at the same time. He was sure more cash had to be in the house. He searched every room upstairs and was lying on the floor in the master bedroom looking under the bed, when to his surprise; he saw another pair of feet on the other side of the bed! He jumped up to find the man of the house standing there with a fire poker in his hand. The homeowner yelled,

"Try and rob me, eh, you bastard," as he swung the poker in the direction of Everton. The poker missed its mark, but gave Everton the opportunity to draw his knife and slash at his attacker. The homeowner swung again wildly, but missed again. Everton took his time and lunged forward stabbing the man in the right side of his chest. The man fell to the floor.

Everton stood over him his eyes went wide as he said, "Be thankful I don't cut your heart out." With that, Everton shoved the blade of his knife into the man's leg making him scream with agony. Everton then made good his escape, out the rear door.

About an hour later, the lady of the house came home. A minute later, she came running out of the house screaming, "My husband's been murdered. Police, Police." In fact, her husband, although wounded, was still alive. Several neighbours had heard the ruckus so came running to the woman's assistance.

Eventually, the police arrived and began their investigation that included searching the area. Later that day, when the report of the robbery arrived at the Police station, one of the detectives mentioned it to Inspector Booth. He told him that he felt it could be Everton Magumba. After reading the account of the robbery, the inspector agreed. This had been a vicious attack on the homeowner, unusual for that type of robbery. The inspector directed his detective to try to find some witnesses who may have seen the culprit entering or leaving the house.

A day after the vicious break and enter, evidence was starting to come in. First, a witness had been located who claimed to have seen a man running away from the scene of the crime down the rear laneway. He had appeared to be a black man of average height dressed in mostly black clothing. Second, Inspector Booth had instructed one of his detectives to compare the knife wound left on the homeowner to that of the numerous knife wounds found on Tony Drummond. What he wanted to discover was any similarities between the knives used in both crimes. The detective also escorted the homeowner to the Coroner's office to have his wound inspected by the pathologist who had done the autopsy on Tony Drummond. After examining his wound, the pathologist determined they were from the same type of knife. The detective, therefore, reported his findings back to Inspector Booth. The evidence collected seemed to point toward Everton Magumba as being the prime suspect in the knifing of both the homeowner as well as the murder of Tony Drummond.

THIRTEEN
COME OUT, COME OUT WHEREVER YOU ARE

Everton Magumba knew he was now a wanted man after his last break and enter. He was angry that the homeowner had come home and caught him in the act. Next time, he would have to be more wary. For now, he had enough money to lay low out of sight for the rest of the month. He knew that the sooner he got rid of Henry Bruce, the better it would be for him. As soon as he killed him, Everton's plan was to travel west away from Toronto, the city where his one and only brother had been murdered. Then, he would go south and toward New York City so he could finally make his way back to London. He dared not go through Halifax, as they would be on the lookout for him.

Everton felt he had to seek out the protection of a local gang operating in Toronto. He was tired of moving from rooming house to rooming house. He knew the gang was an Irish gang and where their hangout was. Everton decided to pay them a little visit to introduce himself. A guard was standing at the front door of the gang's hangout when Everton got there. He told him to take him inside to have him meet the boss man. At first, the guard told Everton to get lost, but after Everton had pulled his big knife from his waistband, the guard did what he was told.

Everton was led into the basement of a four story building, and then shown into a large room where young men were sitting on old thrown out couches. The guard took Everton in front of one man. "This guy wants to talk to you, watch him he has a knife."

But before anything else could be said, Everton jumped on the boss once again pulling out his knife, which he put to the boss's throat and said,

"My name is Everton. I'm going to stay with you for a while."

The man on the couch was taken back and somewhat speechless.

"Let me tell you who I am." continued Everton.

"I come from the roughest gang in London. I was sent here to get some money back that was taken from us, and then kill the man who did it — maybe you heard of him? Tony Drummond." Everton said.

"That was the detective at the Windsor Hotel that was murdered." said one of the gang members.

"That's right, I cut his throat from ear to ear." boasted Everton.

"In that case, I'm Boomer, nice to have you on board. How can we help you?" queried the boss.

Everton sat down next to the boss and explained the whole story to him. He said, "What I need right now is a safe place to hide." Everton told the boss how his brother had been murdered by Tony Drummond, which is why he also had met his end the way he did. Everton then added that he would be happy to help the gang, if they had any enforcement problems because that's what he was good at. He then told them that he enjoyed using the big knife on people's throats.

"We rarely do that here. We only need to beat up our prostitutes to make them work and hand over their money." said the boss.

"But we do have trouble with another gang. They're Italians and connected down in the States." said the boss

"Just a word of warning." explained Everton, "Don't you or none of your men try and do me no good. I've killed many people and a few more means nothing to me."

"Okay, Okay." said Boomer.

With all that being said, Everton picked himself up off the couch and finding another couch in another corner of the room, went and lay down. "Now don't bother me I'm going to rest a while." and went to sleep.

It had been two months since William, Sarah and Roger had arrived from London. Things couldn't have worked out better for all of them. Once, they had started into a proper routine, the house ran smoothly with the dinner meal waiting for everyone when they got home from work and school. The kids got along well and had made numerous friends in the area. Weekends were spent with both families doing activities they loved — fishing, painting, walking, and sightseeing day trips, which everyone enjoyed. Their lives were full and happy. The unpleasantness of the previous two years had almost been forgotten, at least, by all, but Henry. He still worried about Everton Magumba and his whereabouts. Henry also had not heard from the inspector in a while, but was always aware of what was going on around him. The gun was still in the spot Henry had put it, even though, at one point, Emma had wanted to get rid of it.

Thomas and Teresa were doing fine as well. Occasionally, on holidays or special occasions, everyone would get together for a big meal. Thomas enjoyed Henry and William's company, even though, they were younger than him. They were relatives and from over home so had so much in common with him. When all three families got together, there was always a lot of laughing, story telling and, yes, even singing of the old British songs.

All was going just fine, until one afternoon, when Thomas came home from work in a hell of a state. He had been roughed up. His lip was split and he had a black eye.

"What the hell happened to you love!" exclaimed Teresa.

"Oh, God, it's not over yet. I must go see Henry." Thomas said in a worried voice.

"You're not going anywhere until you tell me what happened and I fix those wounds!" shouted Teresa.

Thomas sat down and as Teresa was tending to his wounds, he told her what had happened. He had been walking home from work when that black man jumped out in front of him. "Yes, the man that killed Tony Drummond — the one in Emma's picture. He punched me in the mouth first and then grabbed me by the throat. He pulled a huge knife out and put it to my throat. He wanted to know where Henry was. He kept screaming at me, 'Where did he go after he moved out of your house?'"

I told him that Henry had taken his wife and kids and moved back to London, but I don't think he believed me. He punched me in the eye and told me if I was lying that he would come back. I told him, "You should just leave us alone. We were not involved in the death of your brother. We had nothing to do with it."

Thomas went on to say, "He said he didn't care. He would come back and do more than just hit me. He scared me so much that I had to tell him I really didn't know where the Bruces had gone. He started yelling a bunch of mumbo jumbo at me. I couldn't understand him. It was in another language, but he was furious and out of control. He didn't look well. He seemed out of his mind. Then he just ran off."

Teresa said, "Honey, you can't go to Henry's house. That man might be out there waiting to follow you. He's not stupid. He knows that's the first thing you will do. No, you must go and see that Inspector at the police. Let him go to Henry and tell him."

"Darlin, that's why I married you. You're not only beautiful, but you're smart." exclaimed Thomas

"As a matter of fact, I will go to the police. You stay here. Lock the doors and rest up." said Teresa.

"That's an even better idea." agreed Thomas

Teresa left by way of the back door and then the rear laneway behind the house. She walked a couple of blocks away making sure she was not being followed. Then, she boarded the streetcar for downtown. Once there, it was a short walk to the police station.

Although, she didn't know the inspector's name; it wasn't long before the desk Sergeant was off to find

Inspector Booth. After Teresa had explained what had happened to Thomas, the inspector praised her for her clear thinking and thanked her for coming to the station. Two burly looking detectives then escorted her home. The Inspector also ordered the detectives to search the area and then take up observation of Teresa's home for the rest of their shift, just in case this black madman returned.

The inspector was very concerned because it sounded like Everton was becoming more unstable and dangerous; if that was possible. Meanwhile, the Inspector would take a trip out to see Henry to inform him as to what had transpired. Along the way, he could possibly devise a plan to flush Everton out of hiding. It had been several months since Tony Drummond and Livingston Magumba had been murdered. Everton was, obviously, in hiding but where? The Inspector thought he must be with people that he trusted; otherwise the police would have seen him by now. The Inspector further reasoned that the only people that Everton would trust were people as low as himself — other gang members. He knew that a couple of the plainclothes detectives in his unit had an informant buried deep in the worst Irish gang in Toronto, led by a guy nicknamed 'Boomer'. The inspector would have his men contact the informant to see if the gang was hiding Everton. If they could locate him; then they would raid the location and try to arrest him.

Everton had returned to the gang's safe house where they were hiding him. Boomer was also at the house and wanted to talk to him. Boomer told Everton that he had concerns that there was an informant a 'rat' in his gang. Boomer thought that as repayment for their hiding him;

Everton could help them by finding out who 'the rat' was and disposing of him. Everton agreed that he would be more than happy to get rid of the trash, as he put it. Boomer then gave Everton all the information he had and why he thought there was someone like that in his gang. He told Everton that on several occasions, police had got information that they should not have been able to obtain. Whoever was leaking this information was a danger to everyone in the gang and had to disappear. Boomer went on to say that he had no idea who the rat could be. As it turned out, Everton, who was suspicious of everyone and trusted no one had been noticing things going on within the gang. He had said nothing to Boomer, but he already had several people in mind that smelled like a rat.

Inspector Booth's carriage pulled up outside the Bruce residence. Emma saw him arrive and met him at the door. He was a nice chap and Emma was always glad to see him. She invited him in and offered a cup of tea, which the policeman couldn't refuse.

"So what brings you all the way out here Inspector?" inquired Emma.

"Well to be honest with you there's been trouble. Thomas was roughed up by Everton Magumba." said the Inspector. "Where is Henry?"

"He just stepped out he'll be right back." said Emma.

The Inspector assured Emma that Thomas was on the mend from his encounter with Everton. He thought rather than repeat the whole story again to Henry when he got back that he would wait to tell them both together. Meanwhile, Emma and he could have their cup of tea. The two sat and talked about how Emma's family was doing in

Toronto and she showed the Inspector some of the paintings that she was working on.

"These are quite wonderful. I'll have to pay you to do one of these portraits of me." the Inspector said with a wink of his eye.

"Why inspector, I'd be more than happy to… paint you." Emma said, blushing.

Just then Henry came in the front door so the two painting enthusiasts stopped flirting and got back to the Inspector's visit.

"Hello Henry" said the Inspector.

"Inspector Booth, how nice to see you again, or is it?" Henry asked.

The Inspector sat Henry down and proceeded to tell both of them what had happened to Thomas.

"I knew it!" exclaimed Henry, "Things were going just too well. I had a feeling that something was about to happen. What do we do now?" asked Henry.

Of course, he was concerned about the wellbeing of his great uncle, but the Inspector reassured him that Thomas was well but just needing to recuperate from his encounter with Magumba. The policeman went on to say, "It sounds like Everton is becoming more unstable so could become even more violent. There were two break ins, which I believe Everton was responsible for and in the second break in, he had actually put his knife into the owner's leg."

The Inspector then told the Bruces that he had a plan to try and locate Everton and that if his plan worked it wouldn't be long before Everton would be in custody. He also said, "I absolutely forbid you to try to handle it yourself. You and William must stay completely out of it, aside from taking your normal precautions as you have already been doing. In the meantime, I will have four officers patrol your street until Everton is apprehended. Two officers will be uniformed, but the other two will be in plainclothes. I will have them check in with you when they are in the area." This made Emma feel a little better.

The inspector finished by saying that Teresa had assured him that Thomas would be all right after some rest. He had told her the same as he was telling Henry, which was to stay out of it. He emphasized, "Neither Teresa nor Thomas should try to contact you as it appears that Everton does not know where you live. I want to keep it that way..."

***

Back at the hangout, Everton had devised a plan to flush out 'the rat'. He would tell one of the gang members whom he suspected of being the rat that he was going to break into a jewellery store the next Friday night. He would give the person the location and the time that he was planning on doing it. Then, he planned to be across the street on the roof of another store to see what would happen. If the police showed up, then he would know who the rat was and deal with him. If the police didn't show up, then the second of the two gang members whom Everton suspected would be interrogated at the point of Everton's knife. Friday was two days away, which should give the suspected 'rat' enough time to get word to his police friends. The trap was set. Everton told the man that he suspected about his fictitious jewellery store break in. Everton from the roof of the store across the street had a good view of the jewellery store. Now, he only had to wait until Friday night… That was the easy part.

On Friday night at 10:00, Everton was perched on the roof across the street with full view of the jewellery store. All he had to do now was wait. He had told the suspected 'rat' that he was going to break into the store at midnight, that way he said there would be no pedestrians walking by to bother him. Everton noticed several men milling about in the next block. For the two hours before the appointed time, all was very quiet, too quiet. Then at 12:30, all hell broke loose. Policemen flooded the area to the back and front of the jewellery store. The trap had worked. Everton was proud of himself, but he now had to lay low until the coast was clear before he could get away from the area.

Inspector Booth was waiting back at the police station to hear the results of the raid on the jewellery store. He had to be ready to question Everton about the murder of Tony Drummond as well as about the two break ins and the assault on Thomas Bruce. The Inspector would be truly relieved when this murderer was off the streets behind bars. Then the word came that Everton had not showed up. Booth instantly hoped that Everton had just changed his mind or got scared off. If he hadn't, it meant that the informant at the gang had possibly been found out. If that was the case, the informant's days were numbered. Booth then ordered the plainclothes officer working with the informant to get word to him to tell him to get the hell away from the gang as his cover had possibly been blown.

The next day, when Everton finally returned to the gang's hideout, he let Boomer know what happened, and how he had set up the suspected rat to confirm that he was the traitor. Everton told Boomer to leave the rest to him, as he would kill the pesky rodent.

***

Emma had been arguing with Henry ever since they had received word about Thomas's encounter with Everton. Emma was starting to blame her husband for all that had happened to the family. She was really angry with him as she had never been before. Henry just kept saying how sorry he was and that he never would have thought things would have turned out the way they did. For the first time, she even threatened to leave him and take the kids with her back to London. When she said that, Henry saw red and grabbed her by both arms. She thought for the first time in their marriage that Henry was going to hit her. Instead, he put his big arms around her and whispered, "Please forgive me."

***

Everton was waiting in the shadows of the gang's hideout. Waiting for a certain rodent to show his face. Then, in he walked. His name was Sam and he had been with the gang for about a year, ever since the Italian gang in a dispute had murdered his brother over two of the prostitutes working for their gang. As soon as Sam saw Everton, he knew he had been set up. He was in real danger now. He tried to turn and run, but Everton had put two men on the door to prevent him from escaping. In a loud voice, Everton said, "Sam where are you going in such a hurry, what's the matter, you don't like me?"

"Of course I do," Sam said nervously.

"Oh Sam, that's not true is it? If you liked me, you wouldn't have told the Bobbies where I would be last night…. Right Sam?" said Everton sarcastically.

"I don't know what you're talking about Everton. I never said 'nuthin' to nobody." Sam said defiantly.

Everton walked over to Sam and grabbed him by the back of his hair forcing his head back.

"Let me show you what we do in London to little rats like this guy." said Everton. As soon as he had said it, he took his knife and with one smooth motion slit Sam's throat from ear to ear. Sam dropped to the floor.

"Wrap his body in that blanket and dump him in the Humber River. Go on get on it!" Everton yelled at the two men who had been at the door.

"You heard him… get to it." Boomer yelled.

Everton looked at Boomer and shrugged his shoulders with a big smile on his face and said, "Problem solved, right?"

Boomer didn't know what to think. Part of him was in shock at what had happened. He thought to himself that Everton was quite crazy. No one had ever done anything like that before. If someone needed taking care of, they would just beat him up. That was usually enough of a warning to fix a problem. This was just crazy! Boomer wanted Everton out of the gang … not that he had ever been invited in. He really had just showed up one day and never left. He was truly a dangerous man and Boomer didn't want him there anymore. Boomer dared not say anything to Everton right now. Who knew what he would do. He would have to wait until things cooled down.

Two days passed, before Sam's body was found floating face down in the Humber River. It wasn't long before Inspector Booth's plain-clothes detective positively identified the body as that of his informant, Sam. The Inspector was furious. This murdering coward Everton Magumba had set up the police.

Inspector Booth gave the order for the gang's headquarters to be raided along with every safe house they were known to use. They had to flush out Magumba. He also wanted Boomer arrested and brought in, as well as all the gang members they could find. They had to be interrogated one by one.

Everton had left the gang's safe house the day that he had murdered Sam. He knew he had at least a day before the police found Sam's body and would show up at the hide out. So Everton planned on being on the other side of town when that happened. He found a vacant horse stable in the East end where he could hole up in for a few days undetected, while he made plans for his next move. In the meantime, Everton had a job he had to do. He had to locate the burial site of his brother Livingston. He believed the grave would be in an unmarked city grave. Once he located the grave, he would dig it up under the cover of darkness and place Tony's severed body parts in the grave with Livingston. He would repeat the process again once Henry was murdered.

FOURTEEN
THE HUNT IS ON

Another month had passed by and things at the Bruce home had returned to normal. Thomas had recuperated from his ordeal with Everton. The police were still patrolling the streets around the Bruce home, but Everton was nowhere to be found. All the gang members had been interrogated and two of the men gave statements regarding the murder of Sam, the informant. As a result of these statements, charges were brought against Boomer and another warrant was issued for the arrest of Everton Magumba for murder. Booth had now set up a dragnet over Toronto trying to locate Everton. Police were working over time in the search for this most dangerous suspect.

Everton had spent the last month moving from one hiding spot to another. He had narrowly missed being apprehended when the police searched the stable where he had been hiding. Everton had had enough of the stable, as it was getting colder outside with winter coming on. He had found a house close to a grocery store that he thought was vacant, but when he broke in, he found that there were people still living there. He waited until the couple returned home and then overpowered them and tied them up. He told them he would not hurt them, but only wanted to stay there for a few days. Everton had to get to work and kill Henry before the police caught him.

The couple that Everton tied up in their own house was a young newly wed couple in their late twenties. The man was very thin — not muscular at all. Everton thought to himself that he sure hadn't worked hard for a living so must have come from a family with money. The lady was petite and attractive so Everton enjoyed binding her arms behind her back and thought he would enjoy playing with her later on. Her husband may have to meet the working end of his knife, if he caused him any trouble. The young couple were both petrified they had never had anything like this happen to them before.

Despite what Inspector Booth had told Henry about leaving Everton Magumba to the police, Henry was determined to find him to put an end to all this violence that had been directed toward his family. He thought that if he paid a visit to the gang's clubhouse, he could talk with someone who might know something he could use in his search. Henry wasn't at the clubhouse very long before he met an older man, in his sixties, who the gang let hang around and do small errands for them. He loved to talk making himself sound more important than he actually was. He told Henry that some of the gang members would ask his advice on certain matters, and he would give them his opinion. As soon as Henry mentioned the black man named Everton, the old man's demeanour changed. He told Henry he didn't trust that bastard and that he was dangerous and crazy. The old man hadn't been there when he murdered Sam, but he had heard all about it.

The day after the murder, the old man said that Everton had talked to him about having to get away to hide, but really didn't know where to go. The old man really didn't want to help him, but couldn't help himself. He told him he would be smart to hide in the East end of Toronto, as maybe the police wouldn't look for him out there. Everton told him he would look for a vacant house to break into and hole up for a couple of weeks.

"Oh, and one other thing," the old man said,

"What's that?" asked Henry.

"Everton said he wanted to be really close to a grocery store as he was losing weight." said the old man.

This could be good information Henry had thought to himself. As he headed for home, he thought about the information that he had received and how he could use it. He knew that the 'East end' meant anywhere in Toronto that was east of Yonge Street, which ran north and south in the middle of the city. Henry knew that, at work, there was a large book, which had every business in Toronto in it classified into type of business and its address.

If Henry could get the names and addresses of grocery stores in the East end; then he could go visit each one and ask if a black man had bought anything there. He would get Emma to draw a portrait of Everton based on his description and show it to the proprietors. He would also have to borrow the company bicycle from work to go from store to store. Before too long, Henry had his list and the portrait of Everton Emma had drawn for him. It wasn't bad at all for someone who had never seen him; anyway it was a close enough resemblance.

Henry had obtained a map of the city and had put an 'x' where the grocery stores in the East end were — a total of twelve stores to check. This was going to take time. It took an hour for Henry just to get to the East end by bicycle. Once there, he started checking each store out. It wasn't until grocery store number 10 that Henry got the answer he was looking for.

"Yeah, I remember that guy... What a freak of nature he was!" said the proprietor.

"What do you mean?" Henry queried.

"He was very rude. He was hard to understand, and got mad when I told him we didn't have any goat milk. Anyway, he bought a number of food items, and as he was going out the door he said, 'You wouldn't last long in my country!' Then he walked out." said the proprietor.

"Do you know where he went?" Henry asked.

"No, I was just glad to get him out of my store." the proprietor said.

On the way back home, Henry thought to himself *that's got to be him. But how am I going to find out where he went. The owner of the store said he bought a quantity of food items that should last him for a week or so. That gives me time to make my next plan.* By the time Henry got home, he was exhausted. He told Emma what he had found out. She insisted that he should contact Inspector Booth with this new information, but Henry just said that he would think about it.

Everton knew that the police would watch the area around Thomas Bruce's house. He had to come up with a way of finding out where Henry lived. He decided to let things cool down a bit before going out to the area where Thomas lived and start snooping around again. Everton thought that when he started looking around the West end, he would find a place out there to stay. Meanwhile, he was going to have some fun where he was. He had only had relations with hookers and alike, not a refined pretty lady like he had tied up in the bedroom.

***

Inspector Booth knew that only good police work would result in the arrest of Everton Magumba. He had some of the finest detectives in Canada working on the case, and yet there were still no positive leads. He ordered his best detectives to re-interview all the witnesses including the gang members.

The next day, the Inspector was informed that an old man who hung around the gang's house had been re-interviewed. He had some interesting information. He told the detective that there had been another detective there asking questions the day before. The old man told this detective that Everton had talked to him after the murder and asked his advice about where he should hide out. The old man had told him to go to the East end of town and lay low for a while. The old man also told this other detective that Everton said he was losing weight so wanted to be near a grocery store to buy some proper food.

The Inspector was furious. Who was this other detective that got information like that and hadn't passed it on? He ordered his Sergeant of Detectives to find out who he was and bring him in for an interview. That afternoon, the Sergeant of Detectives reported to the Inspector that he had questioned each one of the men working under him on the case and found no one who had been talking to the old man.

"So who was he then?" the inspector asked rhetorically. Then, it dawned on him 'Henry' that 'son of a bitch' is doing what I told him not to do. With that, the Inspector ordered his carriage to be brought around front. He was going to pay Mr. Bruce a little visit. The Inspector's carriage pulled up in front of the Bruce house and the Inspector was at the front door banging on it within seconds. Emma answered the door and gave the Inspector a nice wide smile

"Why Inspector, how nice to see you again." Emma said coyly.

"Hi, Emma," a nice smile and a wink followed, "Where's that husband of yours!" Booth demanded. Emma knew there was something wrong.

"I'll get him, please come in." Emma said sheepishly.

"Thank you, dear" Booth said. Emma looked again at him and smiled.

Henry came into the parlour and before he could shake the Inspector's hand, the inspector started dressing him down. "What the hell did I tell you? I said to leave it to the police didn't I?" barked the Inspector.

"I know. I'm sorry, but I think I know where Everton may be."

"What! What do you mean?" the Inspector said, starting to calm down.

"Explain yourself…"

Henry went on to tell the inspector about all the grocery stores in the East end and how he had gone around with a portrait that Emma had drawn and showed it to the owners of the various grocery stores. Then he told Booth about the one store where the owner recognized the image in the portrait. Henry told the inspector that he had planned to go back there and watch for Everton to show up. Henry figured Everton wouldn't go back for a few days to a week because he had already bought food.

"Well I'll be a monkey's uncle." said the Inspector. Emma chuckled a bit.

"You've done very well for an untrained man." said the Inspector.

"Why thank you." said Henry.

"Now, I'm going to warn you. You will leave this up to my police force, and if you get involved again; I will have you arrested for obstructing justice. Is that clear Henry?" advised the Inspector.

"Yes, I understand." said Henry.

The inspector then told Henry that his detectives had got the same information from the old man when they re-interviewed him. In other words, they would have arrived at the same conclusion as Henry did. "However," the inspector said, "What would have happened if Everton had seen you at the grocery store? He would have killed you right on the spot, right Henry?" Henry had to agree with the inspector….

"I told you I'll keep you informed." said the Inspector, as he walked out the front door.

***

Everton had decided it was time to leave the house where he was. He had taken advantage of the young lady several times and had thought about killing his two prisoners, but decided to let them live. He would, though, leave them bound up while he made good his escape. He would then head to the West end to finally find Henry. Everton ate a good meal, kissed the lovely lady, and left.

Everton had stolen a large winter over coat with a large collar from the man of the house. If he wore a large hat and pulled the collar of the coat up; one could hardly see his face so could barely detect he was a black man. Dressed in this way, he got on the streetcar and rode it to the West end. Along the way, he was thinking about how to find Henry. Then it came to him. He knew that Henry frequented the Gladstone hotel. This would be perfect because he could rent a room at the Gladstone and spend most of his time in the men's room waiting for Henry to come by for a beer. Before long, Everton had rented the cheapest room in the hotel and was sitting in the corner of the men's beverage room waiting for Henry.

***

The couple, bound up in their own home, were desperately trying to free themselves. The man had rolled across the floor and with his foot knocked over a glass floor vase smashing it. Then, with a broken piece of glass started working on cutting the ropes that were keeping him bound. His wife was of no help to him as she was in shock from the assaults that had been leveed on her by Everton. Finally, the rope gave way and the gentleman was free.

After removing the ropes binding his feet, he went to his wife and undid her ropes to free her. She grabbed him crying uncontrollably.

The first thing on his mind was to get his wife to a hospital. He ran next door and banged on the front door — no answer. He started yelling for help and for the police. Before long, other neighbours were by his side willing to give him assistance. One of the neighbours brought around his carriage and helped the man's wife inside, and then off to the hospital they went. Other neighbours were asked to contact the police to tell them what they had been through and where they were taking his wife.

As luck would have it, the Detectives assigned to watch the grocery store, which was only a half block away, heard the commotion and before long were on the scene obtaining information. One of the Detectives left the scene to go to the station, while two more were on their way to the hospital. The Detective, at the station, burst into Inspector Booth's office with the news of the hostage taking and possible rape perpetrated by Everton Magumba. After obtaining as much information as the Detective could offer, Inspector Booth was on his way to the hospital where the victims were being interviewed.

The male victim was with his wife in the emergency area of the hospital. His wife was suffering from severe shock, cuts and abrasions. They had not determined whether she had been raped, and she was in no shape to say anything. She was constantly crying and occasionally would scream her husband's name in her delirium. He too was being treated for cuts he had sustained while freeing himself.

Inspector Booth arrived at the hospital within the hour and before long was talking to the male victim. The Inspector had with him the portrait that Emma Bruce had drawn for her husband, which he showed to the man. He readily identified the man as the man who had attacked them. The man's wife would not be well enough to talk to the police for several days, if at all in the near future. Booth had a good witness in the husband so he saw no need to interview the traumatized woman. In any event, Everton Magumba was the culprit responsible.

Henry had once again taken the day off work to go to the East end on his hunt for Everton. When William arrived home from work, Henry took him aside and filled him in on what had happened during the day including the visit from Inspector Booth. William told him that he had done a good piece of detective work. The two men were about to walk down to the Gladstone Hotel to have a pint of ale, when Henry thought it might be wiser to stay close to home in case anything happened such as Everton showing up. They decided to relax and sit on the front porch of the house.

Four Muskoka chairs were on the porch, named as they had been designed for cottages in the Muskoka area of Ontario — an area about one hundred and twenty five miles north of Toronto. It was an area of lots of fishing camps and hunting lodges. The two men sat down and started a long conversation reviewing everything that had happened over the last six months. Emma and Sarah came out to the porch to join the men. Even though, the days were getting shorter with the approach of winter; it was still a lovely day and fairly warm. With the women joining them, the topic of conversation soon turned to the future and what each of the couples would like to do with their lives. Little Roger was sitting on the front step listening to the grownups talk.

Emma mentioned that Inspector Booth had told her that he would probably be able to get her a good job on the police force using her drawing skills to help on things like robberies and missing persons.

Henry asked her, "What did you tell him?"

"I said that I might be interested, but let's wait until this problem with Everton sorts itself out." said Emma.

"Booth told me I would be the first one in Canada to do a job like that!" Emma said proudly.

"You would be in the history books, Emma," Sarah said. Then they all chuckled.

"Maybe your Det. Booth could get me a job as a detective. He was really impressed with the work I did trying to find Everton." said Henry.

"I bet he could." said Emma.

"Then again, they don't make much money, do they? William and I could make a lot more with our own Tannery shop. Right William?" asked Henry.

"I bet, we could." replied William.

As they sat and talked, Henry noticed two men walking on the other side of the street. It was obvious to him that the two men were detectives, which was confirmed when one of the men looked over at him and nodded.

Inspector Booth was of the opinion that the suspect would now be hiding out in the West end of Toronto. After attacking the two young home owners in the East end, the inspector thought Everton would want to get this all over with and try to get as close as possible to Henry and get ready to attack. The Inspector thought to himself that it wouldn't be long before this tragic mess would be over.

Booth had flooded the area with his plain-clothes men from Thomas's home to Henry's house. He made sure that the men working near Thomas's house stopped by and talked to Thomas as often as possible as a reassuring factor for Thomas and Teresa who were visibly shaken the last time he had seen them. At Henry's house, he wanted the men to just walk by and not approach the house.

While sitting in the beverage room, Everton could see out onto Gladstone Avenue. He was sure something was going on because he had seen men walking up and down the street in an odd manner. He was sure they must be policemen. If they were, they were almost certainly there to arrest him. He would have to stay out of sight. Everton thought that he had to plan his attack on Henry very carefully. First, it was obvious that a daytime attack would be too dangerous, with all these policemen walking around. He decided to go to his hotel room for the rest of the evening, as there was nothing he could accomplish until tomorrow. Staying in the beverage room too long would draw attention to himself needlessly. No matter how eager he was to draw the blade of his knife across Henry's throat, it would have to wait until tomorrow at the earliest.

The inspector had given one of his detective teams the hand drawn likeness of Everton and asked them to show it around to see if anyone recognized him. An experienced detective nicknamed 'Duke' led the team. His real name was Detective Alexander MacDonald. Duke had the disposition of a mean pit-bull. Once he had caught wind of something, he would not let up until he found what he was looking for. He was one of, if not the best men in the Inspector's group of detectives. Duke had been showing the drawing around to various businessmen and store clerks. One of the people that he showed it to was the clerk at the Gladstone Hotel. Finally, he got a hit! The clerk told 'Duke' that he thought that the man in the drawing was a man who was renting a room on the third floor. The man was a black man and gave the name of Mohammed Mohammed. The clerk said that he spent most of his time in the beverage room, and never spoke to anyone. He just kept to himself. This was the type of information the team had been looking for. The 'Duke' had to be careful. He had to get all the policemen away from the Gladstone hotel. They had to retreat for fear of Everton seeing too many policemen around and getting spooked.

After getting the information on Mohammed Mohammed, the inspector had to act fast. He organized a raid on the hotel for that evening, as soon as it got dark. The hotel itself would be surrounded and no one would be allowed in or out until Everton was arrested. As a secondary precaution, uniformed officers would flood the area for a block around the hotel. In the meantime, the hotel would be under constant surveillance until the raid.

FIFTEEN
VANISHED

There was a knock at the door. Henry opened it to find one of the detectives standing there. He advised Henry that the inspector wanted him to know about the raid on the hotel, which was going to occur within the hour. The detective told him that he and his family were to stay in the house with the doors locked, just in case. Henry was excited to hear this news and had everyone in the family gather in the kitchen area. He made it clear that they were not to leave the house until this was over. They locked the doors and shut and latched the windows.

The Inspector gave the order for his men to move in. The hotel was sealed off, no one other than the police was allowed in or out. The suspect, Everton, was not in the beverage room on the main floor. His passkey was obtained from the front desk and 'Duke' and his men went to Everton's hotel room to search it. They expected Everton to put up a fight when they forced their way into the room, but much to their surprise, Everton was not there. The entire hotel was searched from top to bottom. No Everton! As every room in the hotel was being searched, the desk clerk was re-interviewed by the Inspector. Everton had not been seen since he went to his room the night before. The clerk had ascertained this from other employees on the evening shift. Everton's bed had not been slept in the previous night, so he must have left the hotel some time during the night.

"This guy is like a phantom. Every time, we think we have him in our sights, he disappears." said the Inspector.

"I don't know. I just don't know." the frustrated Inspector said.

Everton had acted on his African intuition, and left the hotel the night before. He had grown concerned about all the plainclothes policemen showing up in the area of the hotel. He got on the last streetcar heading east and rode it to the end of the line. In the morning, he would break into yet another building and hole up for a few days. This time he would be more careful and only break into an abandoned building.

A week went by with no sign of Everton around the hotel or at Henry's home. The Inspector had paid Henry and the family a visit to let them know how the raid had turned out.

"Under normal circumstances, this bugger would have been arrested by now." said the frustrated Inspector.

"He's a bit of a slippery fish, isn't he?" quipped Henry.

"We'll get him. Don't you worry about that!" exclaimed Inspector Booth.

The Inspector told Henry that he was now under orders from his superiors to pare back the investigation, due to the excessive man-hours. He assured Henry, though, that he would keep 'Duke' on the case under his watchful eye.

Booth felt something was going to happen very soon, as it had been dragging on far too long. "Everton has come very close to being arrested on several occasions. It is just pure luck on Everton's part that he is still a free man. I won't rest until I see him swing from the gallows at the Toronto Jail!" the Inspector said slamming his fist down on a table.

That weekend, after everyone had settled into their regular routine again, Henry and William decided to take the kids for a fishing trip on the Saturday. He arranged for Thomas and Teresa to come over to the house to spend some time with Emma and Sarah while they were away fishing, as he didn't want the girls left on their own. While the boys were fishing, Winifred practiced her drawing skills.

Over all, it was a fine day and the boys had caught some lovely big trout for dinner. By the time they returned home, it was dark outside and the kids were exhausted going right to bed after their dinner. Sunday would be spent relaxing and doing odd jobs around the house.

Everton had slipped back into the area and had been watching the Queen Street car, when the men came back from their fishing trip. He followed them to the house on Brock Street and watched them go in. During the night, he forced a basement window open, entered the house and then hid in the basement. He thought to himself, *now I've got this Henry in my sights. I can't wait to draw my knife blade across his throat. Livingston, I will revenge your death my brother and cut off his ear and tongue to silence him in the hereafter*. Everton covered himself with old blankets and waited like a lion hiding in wait in the Savannahs of Africa.

When the Bruces got up, they made plans for the day. The kids were going to take little Roger down to Thomas and Teresa's house. Teresa had invited them down to bake cookies with her. The two women were going to do the laundry and the men would work outside getting the property ready for winter. It was a beautiful day and warm for the fall. It wouldn't be long before the temperature got cooler so the snow wouldn't be far behind. As the men were working on the front of the property, 'Duke' rode up on a bicycle.

"How are you doing, 'Duke'?" Henry asked.

The two men shook hands, and Henry offered him a drink of water, which he accepted. 'Duke' was there to check on the family and to tell them that there was no new information. It was as if Everton had fallen off the face of the earth. Little did they know that Henry was in the worst possible danger he had ever been in, with Everton only yards from where the men were standing…

The detective and Henry chatted for a while and then 'Duke' got back on his bicycle and rode off. The women had taken the washing to the back yard and had begun hanging the clothes on the clothesline to dry. Henry had gone into the house to get more water and, as he was standing in the kitchen, Everton came up from behind him and pushed his knife deep into Henry's chest. Henry cried out and then looked into the eyes of his attacker.

"In the name of my dead brother Livingston, die, die, die, die." Everton yelled hysterically.

Then, before Henry passed out, from the pain, he heard a loud bang and saw Everton's face spurting blood. Then Henry passed out. When Henry came to, he was lying on the floor next to Everton. Standing over them was Emma, the gun still in her hand. Tears running down her cheeks.

"Emma, you've saved my life again." whispered Henry.

"Oh my God, the knife is still in you. You're badly hurt, Henry" said Emma.

William came running into the house and, after realizing what had happened, ran back out the door yelling for help and for someone to get the police. William knew of a doctor that lived several doors away and went banging on his door.

Before too long, the doctor was attending to both Henry and Everton. Both men were severely injured. Henry was the worst off with the blade of the knife having punctured his left lung. He had lost a lot of blood and the doctor really didn't think he would live. Everton had been shot in the back of the head with a small calibre handgun before he could draw his knife blade across Henry's neck. The bullet seemed to have exited out of the right eyeball socket. There was no way of telling how serious the wound was. That would depend on how much damage there was to the brain. The knife was still protruding from Henry's chest and one could hear the air escaping from his lung when he tried to breath.

"The knife has to be left in the chest." The doctor advised, "If I remove it now, the lung will collapse and I think he would bleed to death. Only a surgeon will be able to remove it."

William had sent numerous people by bicycle to get the police and eventually they started to arrive. 'Duke' ran up the front stairs and in the front door

"I can't believe this. I was just here not five minutes before the attack took place. Is the black man dead?" asked 'Duke'.

"No, he'll survive, as long as there is minimal brain damage." said the doctor.

'Duke' reached down and put his handcuffs on Everton, then said, "I'm not taking chances with this guy. Everton Magumba, you're under arrest for the murder of Tony Drummond." said 'Duke'.

"I'm staying right by his side from here until he is in shackles," said Duke.

"Both of these men must get to a hospital fast if we are to save their lives." said the doctor.

When the word got back to police headquarters, two attendants left with the police ambulance bound for Brock Street. Before long, the two injured men were in the back of the horse drawn ambulance, racing toward the Toronto General Hospital. 'Duke' went along for the ride to make sure Everton didn't get away.

Inspector Booth had been contacted at his home and was now racing to the Hospital. Along the way, Everton had become conscious and tried to get out of his handcuffs. When Duke saw this, he punched Everton in the mouth and sent him back to unconsciousness.

"Not on my watch, you murdering bugger." 'Duke' mumbled to himself.

William took Emma down to catch the Streetcar to go to the hospital, leaving Sarah to go to Thomas's house to let them know what had happened. The kids could stay with Sarah and she would bring them back home. Before that, though, the blood on the hall floor would have to be cleaned up.

On the streetcar, William asked Emma how she knew Everton was in the house. Emma told him she had seen him through the back window and then she had snuck in the house to get the gun just as he had stabbed Henry. She told him that she had never fired a gun before and was deathly afraid of it, but she had to shoot because Everton was determined to kill Henry. I just aimed at his head and pulled the trigger.

"You're a very courageous woman." William told Emma.

At the hospital, Henry had been immediately taken for emergency surgery. Performing his surgery was one of the best surgeons in Canada. He lived close to the hospital and was summoned as soon as the severity of Henry's wound had been determined. The operation would take several hours unless Henry passed away. The Inspector arrived on the scene at the hospital and after checking into Henry's condition, went to see Everton. 'Duke' was still by his side and had placed one half of the set of handcuffs on himself.

"Wherever he goes, I go." said Duke.

"Would you like leg irons on him, as well?" inquired the Inspector.

"Yes sir. That would make me feel even better." said 'Duke'.

'Duke' went on to tell the Inspector how he had just spoken to Henry not ten minutes before he had been attacked so that Everton had been there the whole time ... waiting for his chance. Everton was, without a doubt, one of the most dangerous men either men had ever encountered or even heard of. He would be facing a long list of criminal charges including murder, assault, kidnapping, sexual assault and attempted murder, not to mention minor charges like the break and enters and so on.

Emma and William arrived at the hospital and were met by the Inspector who proceeded to update them on Henry's condition. He assured Emma that everything was being done to save Henry, but he was a very sick man. The Inspector then took William aside and asked him what he knew about what had happened. William told him what Emma had related to him about the shooting, at which point, the Inspector praised her for her clarity of thought. She did in deed save Henry's life.

Now, it was only a waiting game until the operation was over. Emma sat quietly knowing that it was going to be a long night. The only good news was that they were still operating, had he died the news would be immediate. If Henry survived the operation, he would be in hospital for months. Emma started to cry, which both William and the Inspector noticed.

"What am I going to do, William? If Henry dies, I'll have nothing to fall back on?" said Emma.

"Don't worry about any of that right now. It's a good thing Sarah and I are here. We will take care of you and the kids while we wait and see about Henry. No matter how long his recuperation takes, we will be here for you." Replied William.

"Thank you, William," Emma said while sobbing.

"I think there might be reward money coming your way, Emma, and don't forget the money that Tony left to you and Henry. Don't worry about anything right now you will be fine." said Inspector Booth.

The doctors had treated Everton's head wound and had told him that he had lost his right eye, but seemed not to have much brain damage. He had nerve damage to his left side and was unable to operate his left arm, but had all his other senses intact. After another couple of days in hospital, he could be moved to the infirmary at the Toronto Jail where he would stay until his trial.

The operation that Henry underwent lasted well into the night. Henry was under anaesthetic, which had only been used since the 1850s, which rendered the operation painless to Henry, but took time to recover from. Emma was in the waiting room with William the whole time. When it was over, the surgeon came out to the waiting room to talk with her. He told her that the operation went better than expected. The knife blade had missed several major arteries, which had they been severed would have been fatal. As it was, Henry was a very sick man. His injuries would take time to heal, but after the healing process, he should live a long life. Henry would be moved to an intensive care unit to be monitored and cared for. Then he would be moved into a room of his own.

William decided to go back to the house and return with Sarah and the kids. By the time they got back, Henry would be in his own room and would have been cleaned up. It was a good idea for the kids to see that their father was alive and going to make it through the ordeal. Thomas and Teresa would probably want to come as well.

Everton had been placed in leg irons as well as handcuffs. A policeman had been placed at the door of his room as a guard. It was explained to the guard that Everton Magumba was the most dangerous man in Canada and that, even when hospital staff entered the room, they should be accompanied and watched over by the guard. The window in the room was to be sealed and locked, and if Everton became conscious; the guard was to sit in the room and watch every move he made. He was under arrest for multiple murders and other serious offences and until he could be removed to a more secure site, such as the Toronto Jail Infirmary, he was to be placed under the highest security risk. A second guard was also placed at the door to Everton's hospital room leaving one guard inside and one outside the door. It was explained to the guard that "Everton WILL TRY TO ESCAPE as soon as he starts to recuperate."

Henry had been moved to intensive care and had become conscious on several occasions. He was able to speak with Emma briefly, before falling asleep. He told her once again that she had saved his life. She just told him she loved him and to go to sleep and get better. Henry was a very lucky man. He had received the best medical attention that could be provided at that time period in medical history.

When he had passed out from the wound in his chest, he did not regain consciousness again until after the operation. Emma would be by his side until he was well enough to be moved again to a private room. The police Inspector had insisted that Henry be put in a private room when he was taken from intensive care, as he need to be guarded, which could not be done if he was in the regular ward.

The Inspector and 'Duke' made frequent visits to Everton's room to make sure the guards were doing as they were instructed and that the criminal was not up to any tricks. They even had the guards search the room and remove anything that could be possibly used as a weapon. The nurses were instructed not to go near the patient unless one of the guards was standing by her side. At first, the nurses objected to this show of force, but when it was explained how dangerous this man was they understood.

At the scene of the crime, detectives had pieced together how Everton had accomplished his surprise attack. They found the broken basement window that Everton had crawled through. Then they found the hiding spot in the basement where he had waited for the right moment to attack. Upstairs, a drawing was made of the area where the attack had taken place and a blood splatter diagram was made. All of this would be used later in court at Everton's trial. Attention had to be paid to every detail. A schematic drawing would then be made of the whole house so that a model could be made and presented at trial. This would offer the court a complete and accurate picture of the crime scene. Schematic drawings had already been made at the hotel where Tony had been murdered and all the evidence at that crime scene had been collected ready for trial.

Within forty-eight hours, Everton had received further treatment for his head wound. Some of the feeling had come back in his left arm, but it was still not of any use. He was now well enough to be transferred to the Toronto Jail infirmary.

Henry was coming into consciousness more frequently and was able to talk, although, there was a lot of pain when he tried to breathe deeply. Henry had been moved to a private room and would stay there until Everton Magumba was behind bars. Emma and the children had been in to see Henry several times since he had been moved to his private room. The children were very upset at first; but after Henry assured them that he would be back home in no time, this calmed them and lessened the worry they felt for him. Emma had spent most of her time with Henry, and had seen his gradual improvement over the past two days.

They had talked briefly about the attack. Emma told Henry that she had no idea where he had come from, until she had learned from the Inspector that he had broken into the basement and hidden himself down there until he attacked. Emma told her husband that he would have been dead, if Everton had continued the assault. She said, "It was lucky that I found the trigger and squeezed it hard enough for the gun to go off. Actually, the damn thing scared the hell out of me. I didn't think it would be that loud. Can we maybe get a quieter gun?" Emma and Henry both chuckled at that, until Henry winced in pain.

Everton was now starting to realize how much trouble he was in. Even worse, he now realized that he had failed in his bid to kill Henry, and that he had been shot in the head before he could run his knife blade across Henry's throat. He became even more upset when he realized that he would never be able to revenge his dead brother. He swore to himself that somehow he had to try again. However, right now, he was far too weak to even think about it. He was just starting to get used to his limitations. His right eye was gone, but he still had one good eye. His real worry was his left side. He had not tried to walk yet, but he expected he would have great difficulty. He was able to use his left arm, but with great limitation as well. He also had bad headaches that now occurred every day since he was shot. Everton too realized that he had a very long way to go to recuperate from his injuries.

Inspector Booth was able to report to his superiors that Everton Magumba was now under arrest for murder and that he was being held in the Toronto Jail Infirmary. Booth had given interviews to several newspapers, including some from out of town. An English newspaper had interviewed the Inspector wanting to know if Magumba was *Jack the Ripper so* Inspector Booth had sent correspondence to the London Police Criminal Investigations. He offered them all the information regarding the cases that Toronto would be going to trial on with Magumba. The Inspector offered the assistance of the Toronto Police Force after Magumba had been tried on the charges he faced in Toronto.

The Toronto Jail Infirmary, where Magumba was being treated was almost forty years old. It was a fairly modern facility and being part of the jail building was very secure. Inspector Booth had put the Jail officials on notice, that the prisoner they now had in their custody was the most dangerous man in Canada. The Inspector requested that this prisoner be put under the highest security watch possible. The jail officials complied by putting Magumba under double guard. In particular, he was also not allowed near any of the other prisoners. The only utensil he could eat his meals with was a spoon. He was also shackled at all times.

Both Magumba and Henry Bruce were being taken care of medically. It would be months before either man was well enough to get to his feet in a normal manner. Once healthy again Magumba's trial for the murder of Tony Drummond could start.

SIXTEEN
THE TRIAL

Over the next four weeks, Henry had his problems. First, the wound in his chest started bleeding again. It became necessary for him to have another operation to find the bleed and repair it. Next, an infection set into the wound. Operating rooms were not very clean places, and certainly were not sterile. If a wound became infected, Carbolic Acid was used to try to kill the infection. Eventually, the infection subsided and the wound started to heal again. It was a long battle for Henry. Some days were better than others, and the set backs made Henry's recuperation take even longer. The doctors told Emma that any one of these infections could kill Henry.

Everton's recovery had taken a setback as well. As he had minor brain damage, it was enough to make him start having serious *Grand Mal* seizures that could possibly kill him. The only treatment was opium-based drugs like Laudanum. This drug, however, was so powerful that it basically kept Everton sedated while he took it. No surgical procedures had been developed as yet to try to stop the seizures. Everton's only hope was that as his brain healed from the gunshot wound; the seizures would subside on their own.

Inspector Booth was receiving daily reports on both Henry and Everton. He, in turn, would send updates to the Crown Attorney who would be prosecuting at Everton's trial. The Inspector and 'Duke' would also visit the two patients in their respective hospital or infirmary rooms. The owner of the bookstore where Emma worked allowed her to take every other afternoon off work to visit her husband. These visits helped Henry immensely because of the infections he was fighting off. Her visits seemed to make him stronger and more able to cope.

The inspector had also been corresponding with his counter part in London. There was a possibility that the two Magumba brothers together could have committed the murders attributed to *Jack the Ripper*, but there was no evidence or proof to base a case on. If Everton was found guilty of murder in Toronto, there was no doubt that he would hang for the offence. Inspector Booth felt that this would stop the murders on both sides of the ocean for good.

Inspector Reese, of Scotland Yard, had written Inspector Booth and told him of a new technology that was being introduced in England, called fingerprinting. Basically, no two people's fingerprints are the same. They are unique to each person. Fingerprints were the ridges on the pad of each finger and the palm of the hand. They are left behind on smooth surfaces such as glass, metal and finished wood by leaving a deposit of oil in the shape of the fingerprint ridges. When the fingerprint is left behind, it can be seen with the naked eye, but to preserve it, a powder must be used to 'lift' the print and transfer it to a clear piece of cellophane, and then to glass. It can then be compared to other fingerprints of suspects. Only a specially trained fingerprint expert can 'lift' the print to compare it to other prints. Fingerprint technology was gaining respectability in London and would soon be used in courts of law to prove identification. If Inspector Reese had a full set of Everton's fingerprints, he could compare them to prints found at the London murder scenes, if there were any.

It took a month for Everton to become well enough to stand trial. Everton had been undergoing treatments for his seizures to keep them under control. The doctors had experimented with numerous combinations of drugs until they found the right combination that stopped the seizures. One of the reasons he was given a lawyer to represent him was because one of the drugs he was on was opiate based. This had a side effect of making Everton drowsy. It had been determined by the doctors at the jail infirmary that Everton was well enough to stand trial. So, on Monday, October the 1st, 1892, Everton Magumba stood before a judge on the first day of his preliminary hearing. He was charged with premeditated murder in the 1st degree. He, of course, could not afford a lawyer, so the court assigned a lawyer to represent him. When arraigned on the charges and asked how he pleaded guilty or not guilty? Everton pleaded not guilty.

As Henry was still in hospital recuperating from the injuries inflicted on him by Everton, Emma became the first witness at the hearing. She was asked to explain why her family had to move to Toronto. In her evidence, she explained what had happened to her husband, Henry, and the gang in Tower Hamlets back in London. She explained how they had fled London, and come to Toronto to escape the gang and how the victim in this trial, Tony Drummond, had followed them here. She related how Henry had confronted him as soon as he came to Toronto and how she had hit him in the head to protect her husband. Emma told how Tony, eventually, convinced them that even though he had been ordered by the gang's boss to come to Toronto to kill the Bruce family, he had changed his mind and had decided to stay in Canada and not harm them. Tony had agreed not to harm the Bruces if they would help him get re-established here in Canada. The Bruces had agreed to this.

Emma also told the court that the next time her husband Henry had seen Tony was about two weeks later. This was because Henry's uncle Thomas had seen two black men hanging around his house. He thought they might have been sent to cause Henry harm. Henry went to advise Tony and together they came back to try and locate the two black men. Emma also identified Everton as being the person who attempted to murder her husband and the man who she shot in the head to save her husband's life.

Thomas Bruce took the stand next and testified how the defendant Everton was one of the two black men who had been watching his home on Gladstone Ave.

Inspector Booth was next to testify in this mini trial. After he had given his evidence, it was clear to the presiding judge that there was more than enough evidence to go to trial by judge and jury. The preliminary hearing was stopped at that point and a date for trial set in November 1892. This new trial date would hopefully give Henry enough time to recuperate from his injuries, at least to the point, where he could testify. Inspector Booth had been asked by his counterpart at Scotland Yard to notify them when a date for Trial was set. This would give them the opportunity to have one of their officers in court to observe the proceedings.

Henry had been gaining strength. He had fought off the infections that had been threatening his life. He was a very lucky man to be alive, but was getting well enough that he would be able to return home in a week or so. The homeowner that Everton had knifed in the same way wasn't doing as well as Henry. He was having a harder time fighting off the infections and could still succumb to his injuries, only time would tell.

Inspector Booth had compiled enough evidence to charge Everton, not only with the murder of Tony Drummond, but also with the murder of Sam Smith, the informant in the Toronto gang, as well as the attempted murder on Henry and the homeowner. Other charges of rape, wounding, forcible confinement, break and enter and theft could be laid. All of these charges could be proceeded with, if there were no conviction on the Tony Drummond murder charge.

It would be very costly to the province to try to go to trial on all of these charges. If a conviction was secured in the present murder trial, then there was a very good possibility that the death sentence would be imposed on Everton, which would render all the other charges as redundant, and so a waste of money to pursue.

The new trial date for Everton was set November the 10th 1892. It promised to be a very interesting trial and garnered attention from not only across Canada, but most of the free world. Henry had been released from hospital and was recovering nicely at home. The homeowner that Everton had knifed in the chest during the break in, unfortunately, had died of his wounds, which just added another charge of murder to be faced by Everton.

Everton had been moved into solitary confinement from the infirmary at the Toronto Jail. On two occasions, he had attempted to escape custody, by attacking his guards. Prison officials also took the unusual step of ordering him to remain in leg shackles, even when he was in solitary confinement. When the time came for his transfer to the court jail, he would remain in leg irons as well as a straight jacket that was to be kept on him throughout his trial.

It took the Crown and the Defense about a week to choose the members of the jury. On the 10th of November, the trial was set to start. The first witness was Henry Bruce. His evidence was expected to take three days; however, there were continuous outbursts from Everton when Henry was trying to talk. Everton called him a murderer and he would avenge his dead brother, then he would recite a bunch of incoherent mumbo jumbo that no one could understand. At least four times, the trial had to be stopped and Everton warned about his outbursts. If he continued, he would be removed from the courtroom and defended by his lawyer without him being present. Of course, it happened several more times. The judge had no choice but to have Everton removed from the court. Once court had resumed, Henry was clear to complete his evidence. There had been questioning from the Defense Attorney, but there had been no real issues uncovered. Other witnesses gave evidence until all of the Crown's case had been presented. It was now the Defense's turn to offer evidence.

Everton had no friends to stand up for him and the Defense could find no credible witnesses to give evidence on his behalf. As a result, the Defense Attorney chose to call no witnesses. The only witness he could have possibly called was Everton Magumba himself. This would have only made the case against him stronger; the Defense was forced to offer no witnesses and concluded his defense.

Final statements were given by both Crown and Defense. In his closing arguments, the Crown called Mr. Magumba a killer for hire, a violent man who would stop at nothing to get what he wanted. The butcher knife was shown to the jury again after it had been admitted as evidence. The Crown told the jury to look at it, as it was the weapon that the accused had used to murder Tony Drummond by slitting his throat. The weapon was as vicious as the owner. The Crown related that there was a trail of blood shed left by the defendant ever since he landed in Canada. The Crown went on to say that the death of Livingston Magumba may or may not have been the catalyst for Everton's hatred for Tony Drummond, yet at no time did he report the death of his brother to the police. Instead, he left him at the bottom of a well to rot.

The Defense Attorney said that Everton was also a victim in this case. He said that after the death of his brother, he lost all sense of control over his actions. His actions became like those of a mentally disturbed man. This man was not in control of what he was doing at the time of the offence. After both sides had been heard from, it was then the duty of the judge to inform the jury about all of the evidence that they had to consider. I Ie then charged the jury with the responsibility to find the defendant guilty of murder as charged or not guilty. The second part of his charge to the jury was to inform them that if a verdict of guilty was found, then what should the penalty be. The Jury had the power to determine sentence, either death by hanging or life in prison without parole. The Jury was then excused to deliberate their verdict.

The Jury was led out to the deliberating room, as the judge called for a recess until the Jury had reached a verdict. Inspector Booth, along with the Inspector from London, had conversations with the Crown Attorney. The Crown expressed his view that he felt Everton would be hung before the year was out. Inspector Booth agreed, meaning of course that the trial had gone very well.

Henry asked the Inspector how long it could take. Booth answered that he didn't know as it depended on the jury. It could take an hour or days. Everyone would have to wait and see. Henry was advised to wait around until the end the normal hours of court, which meant four o'clock, after that he should go home and wait. The Inspector would send for them when the verdict was ready to be read.

Early the next morning, an officer came to the door at the Bruce's home. He informed them that a verdict had been reached, and that court would reconvene at ten o'clock. The Bruces, Emma and Henry, got ready to go quickly and were soon on their way to court. Once there, Inspector Booth met them so they asked him what he thought.

Inspector booth answered, "Hopefully, he's guilty, but we will only know once the verdict is read."

The judge came into the courtroom to reconvene the trial, first by calling in the Jury. The air was full of suspense as the Jury was ushered in and seated. The judge asked the Jury Foreman to stand. Then, he asked him if the jury had reached its verdict. The Foreman responded that they had and handed the verdict on a piece of paper to the judge. The judge looked at it and then asked the Foreman what the verdict to the charge of murder in the 1st degree was. The Foreman cleared his throat and then said, "We, the Jury, find the defendant Everton Magumba guilty as charged." With that, there was cheering and clapping from the audience, in the body of the court. The judge banged his gavel down several times to regain order in the court.

He then asked Everton to stand and asked him "Before you are sentenced is there anything you wish to say?"

Everton replied, "I am my brother's keeper. I must avenge his death if God gives me the chance. Your court means nothing to me. I laugh at you. You are nothing."

With that the judge banged his gavel again and then turned to the Jury Foreman and said "As to sentence to the offence of murder in the 1st degree, have you come to a decision?" the judge asked.

The Foreman replied, "Yes, your honour, we find that the defendant should receive the maximum sentence allowed in this offence."

The judge thanked the Foreman and the Jury for their decisions and then turned to the defense and had them stand for sentence.

The judge said, "I concur with the verdict handed down by the Jury. I have heard all of the evidence that was offered by the Crown. I agree with the evidence in its accuracy and the weight that the Jury has attributed to this evidence. I find that the accused in this case was in fact a murderer for hire. I also feel that the public is in danger every minute that this man is on the face of the earth. I, therefore, also agree with the Jury's verdict in favour of capital punishment in this case. I therefore sentence you Everton Magumba to be taken to the Toronto Jail Gallows where you will be hung by the neck until you are dead. May God have mercy on your soul."

Again the audience erupted with cheers and clapping. The judge banged his gavel and declared the trial over and then left the court. Everton was livid. He started yelling at the judge and the Jury threatening to kill them all when he got free. The guards led him out of the courtroom; he could be heard all the way down to the cell area yelling at the top of his lungs.

Once outside, Henry asked the Inspector when the execution would take place, and could he and Emma attend the execution. The Inspector advised that the date of execution would be set by the judge's order for execution. And, "yes, he and Emma would be able to attend it if they wanted to."

The Bruces returned home, finally, this whole ordeal was almost over. That night, there was a celebration at the Bruce's home; everyone was there including Inspector Booth and Detective 'Duke' Macdonald. Henry gave a thank you speech thanking everyone for their help during the trying times that they had been through. In particular, he also thanked Emma for saving his life. Inspector Booth told Henry that he would be in touch with him as soon as the execution order was issued by the judge giving the date and time of execution. He anticipated the execution would take place well before Christmas.

The execution would be held at the Toronto Jail. The gallows would be set up in a grassy area in the center courtyard of the prison. The prison gave out invitations to city officials and other government officials for the macabre event and those who couldn't get an invitation of entry would stand on chairs or ladders to see over the prison wall. While awaiting his execution, Everton would be locked in a three foot by two foot cell. He would only be allowed out for less than one hour a day, under heavy guard and was always kept in leg irons. As he had no relatives nearby to claim his body, Everton would be buried in the Jail cemetery.

Inspector Booth had sent a note to Henry and Emma informing them that the judge had written the execution order dated for December the 10th 1892, at one o'clock pm. Along with the note were invitations allowing the Bruces' entry to the area of the jail where the execution would take place. They would be seated in the first row closest to the gallows.

Emma greeted the news with trepidation. She had never actually seen anyone die before. Henry told her this was the only way they could put an end to the whole sordid affair. After the execution, their future would look bright and promising. Upon thinking about it, she finally agreed with Henry. Somehow, she knew that if she didn't see this awful man die on the gallows she would be constantly looking over her shoulder expecting to see him again.

On December the 10th, Emma and Henry were seated before the gallows. A crowd of about twenty dignitaries and city officials were in attendance. At ten minutes to one o'clock, Everton Magumba was led from the jail to the gallows. The hangman went up the stairs first, followed by the minister, and then Everton followed by the warden of the jail and two guards. As his legs were shackled, it took time for Everton to climb the stairs. The minister gave him his last rights, and when asked if he had any last words, Everton spit at the hangman. A black hood was placed over his head, the rope placed around his neck and tightened. The Warden read the order of execution and then at one o'clock, the hangman released the trap door. Finally, the nightmare was over.

The execution of Everton Magumba was a violent way to end a life. Emma was traumatized for weeks afterwards. Henry was less affected by the brutality of the event, having seen violent death at the docks in London. Both Emma and Henry would never forget this part of their life story. Together with their friends, Sarah and William, the following years proved to be very productive. Henry and William started the tanning business they had dreamt about. Emma had started a new job with the Toronto Police Department as a sketch artist. Winifred completed her grade school education at the top of her class. She went on to attend the University of Toronto receiving a Bachelor of Arts. She also attended the School of Art to further her painting. Roland graduated with honours and eventually became a criminal lawyer.

'Jack the Ripper' was never caught. Could it be that Tony Drummond was 'The Ripper', or was it the Magumba brothers? Or was it all three? I guess we will never know……

ABOUT THE AUTHOR

Stephen A. Pease is a Canadian author and retired police officer. He grew up in Toronto, Ontario, and signed up for the Canadian Army Reserve when he was sixteen. In 1973, he joined the Toronto Police Force, where he remained for thirty-four years, working mostly as a Detective Constable. Following his retirement, he began to explore his passions for history and writing, spending several years researching his genealogy and putting it into words. Upon discovering that his relatives lived in the same borough as Jack the Ripper during the nefarious killer's active years, the author was inspired to fuse fact with fiction in his first book. Engima in Whitechapel is a compelling historical crime and adventure novel that combines Stephen's detailed research, his imagination as a writer, and his experiences as a detective in the urban sprawl of Toronto. He now resides in Bobcaygeon, Ontario, with his wife Linda. Together, they have four children. He currently spends his time writing and enjoying the surroundings of his peaceful town.

CPSIA information can be obtained
at www.ICGtesting.com
Printed in the USA
LVHW090119010419
612387LV00005B/17/P

9 781525 513640